MURDER AT THE GARDEN FAIR

Berkshires Cozy Mystery

ANDREA KRESS

© 2022

Created with Vellum

Chapter 1

Our world is constructed with stereotypes. Men are strong, women are weak. Men seek power, and women support them. Men are rational, women are emotional.

We've all grown up with these models of behavior. And how wrong they can be.

You would think that a traditional town like West Adams, Massachusetts, would embody these conventions, and you would be right in theory. But then, someone steps over the line and—whether it be a man or a woman—it's as if the universe were undone.

But I'm getting ahead of myself. I should explain that I, Aggie Burnside, have been a resident of the aforementioned town for the past twelve months, getting used to the local accent, the rhythms of daily life and working as a nurse for Doctor John Taylor. But I am also a keen observer, very much like my landlady, Miss Manley. Come to think of it, I may have honed those skills living with her and being present at her weekly tea group where all manner of conversations were present.

Not all manner. These were a group of run-of-the-mill, middle-class women who grew up in the Berkshires, many on farms, some in the town, but all with that particular grit that defines a New England Yankee. Strip away some of the humble veneers, and a stronger substance lies underneath.

This all became clear to me as summer approached and along with it so many changes. The children were antsy when Mother's Day came and went with an uncharacteristic warm spell. It foreshadowed a long and happy vacation from school, but that was at least a month away. My daily walks in the woods behind Miss Manley's house were highlighted by the sudden leafing out of the deciduous trees, the increased birdsong and the ferns unfurling in the underbrush.

Soon my parents would be coming up for a visit from Pelham, New York, that model suburban community where I had grown up before going to nurses' training in New York City and meeting my classmate, Glenda Butler. It was she who came from West Adams and, following the death of her mother, relocated there, a bit unhappily at being in a small town by herself to sort things out. She never did finish her nursing program and married Stuart, Miss Manley's nephew whom she had known most of her life. Her change in status led her back to Manhattan, where her husband was a partner in a publishing firm, having spent his previous years churning out men's adventure novels.

So much had changed in the past year since I had first arrived. Glenda now had baby Douglas to look after, John and I had developed a romantic relationship with a few bumps along the way, and many strange people had decided to either vacation in or try out West Adams while they figured out the rest of their lives.

Oh, and there had been a murder or two. More on that later.

Glenda had been renting her house adjacent to Miss Manley's and the property was not currently rented. One of the folks who had moved into the area with high hopes of making a go of a strange enterprise was Farley Dexter, a bohemian sort of man who had purchased a nearby farm and employed people down on their luck to help him with a mushroom-growing project. Two of these folks, Mrs. Nelson and her daughter, Joanna, had recently left the farm penniless with a new baby in tow. They were now ensconced rent-free in Glenda's house waiting for the next opportunity to present itself. It was still hard times, and I never did understand what skills or professions either of the women had before becoming, essentially, indentured servants on Dexter's farm. Now, they somehow made do either gleaning or, in the case of Mrs. Nelson, cleaning homes and doing other odd jobs in the brief time before they moved on to work for Reverend Lewis and his wife.

It was a strange arrangement, and I felt sorry for their predicament but was limited in my ability to assist them. Miss Manley already had Annie, who came daily to cook, clean, wash and press my nurse's uniform. I was used to things changing suddenly, and late May and early June were a glorious moment of calm before my family was dragged into an ugly murder and the events that upended the town and the entire county.

Chapter 2

It was a pleasure to sit down to breakfast in Miss Manley's dining room each morning, the meal prepared to perfection by Annie, an amazing cook and stupendous source of local gossip. What was strange is that the telephone didn't ring all that often, meaning the information wasn't transmitted that way. Her most frequent visitor was the Reverend Lewis's maid, Elsie, and they each had their fingers on the pulse of the town, the events and gossip that the rest of us only learned of later. One source of information was, of course, Officer Reed, who was sweet on Annie and took any occasion to stop by the kitchen and take a cup of coffee and a slice of cake and share the latest tidbit. He was Tom Reed, but everyone called him Officer Reed, and I wondered how long it would be before he asked Annie to get married. She had a full life caring for her parents and some siblings besides her job with Miss Manley, yet I suspected she would ditch both in a moment if it meant a permanent home with the policeman.

That morning we were treated to apple fritters and eggs, and I congratulated myself on staying trim by taking an afternoon walk each day, a therapeutic respite from a long day's work: John's practice in neighboring Adams in the morning and West Adams in the afternoon. Annie was busy in the kitchen, baking all sorts of goodies for the tea group that would assemble that afternoon in the sitting room. I was looking forward to the treat as well as the latest tidbits from the women who collectively knew every detail of what was going on in town.

"I heard Doctor Mitchell wants to sell his house in Adams," Miss Manley said. "His wife, Dora, told me about it."

That was a shock. Doctor Mitchell had given his practice there to John although he retained the building, since the second-floor housed paying tenants. If he sold the house, the new owner might not wish to retain a physician's practice on the first floor and that would necessitate a change of location.

"I wonder if John knows?" I asked. "If not, I'd better tell him."

"I'm sure Doctor Mitchell would have said something. Perhaps it was Dora's wishful thinking that they could unburden themselves of the property. Not that it's much to maintain, I wouldn't think."

My mind was whirling with alternatives. If he closed down the Adams practice, would those patients come to him here in West Adams, just a short drive away? At least he wouldn't have to maintain two offices, not to mention the inconvenience of the daily commute and the scheduling issues I had to juggle to make sure folks turned up at the correct location. His financial situation had been tight until recently and with the Depression, people were still careful about spending money. Unfortunately, medical care was now often seen as a less necessary expense until the pain or discomfort got too bad, and then people presented with more complicated issues.

But a new office in Adams might not be a bad thing. There seemed to be several vacant spots right along the main thoroughfare where his shingle could be more prominently displayed. There was even a three-story structure, the Professional Building, where an attorney, an accountant and a dentist already had offices. That might be a feather in John's cap!

"Aggie, I can see that your brain is going at full tilt," Miss Manley said with a smile. She was an expert at reading other people's expressions. Either that or mine were a bit too obvious.

"Yes, a force of habit. Any time there is a change, there is an opportunity," I said, something I had heard someone else say once.

"You know Doctor Taylor has a sterling reputation in both places and he'll work something out," she said.

I excused myself to get ready to go to work, the shortest commute imaginable, just across the back garden, down the side of the Lewises' house and there to the door to John's office.

"Good morning," I said, keeping the sweater on over my uniform since we would be leaving for Adams shortly.

"Ready in a minute," he said from his office, gathering up some papers from the desk.

What a pleasure to see him each day, his broad smile and warm eyes, his enthusiasm for his work and obvious delight in seeing me.

"Onward," he said, picking up his medical bag and a briefcase as I took up the appointment book that shuttled back and forth with us from one office to the other, since patients might call at either location.

I decided not to say anything on our short trip and waited for him to tell me about Doctor Mitchell's situation, but he was quiet, too. He parked in front of the building located just off the main street in Adams and paused to look at it.

"Anything you care to tell me?" I asked.

"Aggie, I have the unsettling feeling that the women of West Adams know everything already."

"Such as?" I tried to appear innocent of information.

"Doctor Mitchell is tired of being a landlord. More like Mrs. Mitchell, from what I know of their relationship."

We mounted the steps to the porch, and he unlocked the door.

"I don't know how much longer we'll be in this location."

"Is that such a bad thing?" I asked. "Aside from the medical equipment that came with your rental, which I'm sure Doctor Mitchell would be more than happy to sell to you."

He looked at me with surprise. "Your mind certainly adapts quickly to the shifting circumstances of life."

"Of course," I said. "What else can one do? What is it *you* want to do?"

"I like this place. It's very comfortable. Acquiring this location and the practice made the transition easy for the local patients and gave them a level of assurance, knowing Doctor Mitchell approved."

"But?" I asked.

He tapped his finger on the end of my nose. "Just wait and see." He led me into his office, opened the briefcase and pulled out a stack of papers. "I'm going to strike while the iron is hot and ask Doctor Mitchell if he will sell the property to me."

I was dumbstruck. How was he going to be able to buy another property? He already owned the house and office in West Adams and complained about the lack of funds. And then add another burden to his financial issues?

"I'm going to get a business loan to buy it. A mortgage."

"Oh," was all I could manage to say.

"Someone gave me a personal introduction to Mr. King, who is the president of the bank here and he seemed an amenable fellow. Surely the banks are eager to get their money moving in the community again after these several slow years."

"Do you think you can afford it?" I almost said 'we,' since we had an understanding and I was always averse to loans or owing money.

"My thinking is that I would keep renting out the upstairs apartment and that would help pay for the mortgage—or even cover it—depending upon the terms I could get. Usually, when you get a business loan, there is some cash up front that could go to getting some additional equipment or modernizing the place."

I looked around and realized it was a bit outdated but perfectly functional. Well, it wasn't my money, after all.

"I've got an appointment with Mr. King this morning."

This was moving very quickly, and I checked the appointment book to make sure that there wouldn't be a disappointed patient. But all was clear.

"Well, good luck," I said, catching his enthusiasm. What I had initially thought was a pokey country practice was growing rapidly.

THE MEETING WENT WELL, and John was all smiles and good humor the rest of the morning, telling me what an excellent fellow Mr. King was, intelligent and encouraging. And in addition to being a bank president, he was one of the three Berkshire County Commissioners.

"It seems you have made a significant contact in the community," I said. I was dying to ask him how large a loan he had asked for but hesitated. It was in one sense none of my business. At least, not yet. The other reason for holding back was that I was afraid if he told me, I might inadvertently yelp in terror. As I said, I was not comfortable with debt.

My father's long recuperation from injuries in the Great War had put my mother into a state of constant worry about money that never relented despite our financial status being reinstated. That little crinkle of concern between her eyes whenever there was a conversation about a big purchase had left its mark on me and, as a result, I was probably overly cautious about expenditures.

In the afternoon at the West Adams office, a mother brought two children in with pink eye, that highly contagious infection that was easily treated but would necessitate them staying home from school. The children thought that was a happy diagnosis, the mother not so much. Otherwise, we had the run-of-the-mill general practitioner's assortment of ailments that day. A farmer appeared with a burn that had become infected, simply because it hadn't been properly cleaned and bandaged in the first place. Miss Smith, the nicer of the two Misses Smith who operated a clothing store on the main street, complained about stomach aches that came and went but could not be specific about describing them.

"Are these sharp pains, dull aches, consistent or intermittent?" John asked.

"Yes," was her answer.

What followed was a rundown of her usual diet, sleep habits and bowel movements, which pointed to nothing specific. I had noticed it was not unusual for patients to say they didn't feel well but couldn't express the sensations or make any sense of linking it to other habits or behaviors. In Miss Smith's case, John suggested she keep a list of the things she ate and drank for a few days and perhaps that would point to the cause. Since all her vital signs were normal and she hadn't said that it interfered with her work or life, it was about the best he could do. Sometimes just a visit to the doctor and a sympathetic ear made milder issues subside over time.

After she left, I asked him, "Do you think she might have an ulcer?"

"Why do you suggest that?"

"Have you met her sister?" I asked.

That got a laugh. "Oh, yes. The other Miss Smith."

The last appointment of the day was a house call for a case of suspected chickenpox. Poor child and poor mother having to tend to him, if that's what it was, and mothers were usually adept at diagnosing that childhood disease.

"I'll see you tomorrow, Aggie," John said, bending to kiss me on the cheek. "You don't want to be late to the tea party next door, after all."

I looked at my watch. "Information central is what I would call it." After he left, I locked up and turned the lights off to enjoy the weekly news updates that were too local and often too personal to be found in the daily **Berkshire Eagle**.

As I walked through Miss Manley's back garden and past the French windows, I could see the weekly event was in full swing, with a level of conversation that could be heard outside. Through the back door, I surveyed the kitchen's enamel tabletop to see if there were additional cookies available, but it was clear. There must be a full house, I surmised. Opening the swinging door from the kitchen into the hall the noise was surprising for what was usually a sedate group. What caused such excitement?

The Garden Fair, of course. The annual local event of great anticipation, participation and competition. I slipped into the sitting room and sat at the far end since attendance was at an all-time high. I smiled to Miss Manley, who nodded her head as I took a seat next to Mrs. Rockmore, who, although paying close attention to the lively conversation, made room for me on the loveseat.

"We can finalize the committee assignments now or have a separate meeting," Mrs. Proctor said with enough subtle force that would bear no dissent. She was almost as tall as I but with a broader, stronger frame.

"Of course, now," Miss Olsen said, seated next to her mentor. I knew Miss Olsen lived with her parents and that her father ran the local hardware store, but I didn't know how a young unmarried woman fit into this social group.

"We have a list of the committees from last year—thank you, Miss Manley, for providing them—and I'll read them off. If anyone has an idea for an additional function or committee to support it, you'd better be ready to chair it!" Mrs. Proctor gave a steely smile that meant she wasn't joking.

"Who did the prize ribbons last year?" Mrs. Strathern asked.

"I did," Mrs. Myers said, tucking her chin in, a little abashed at the attention.

"I thought they were lovely," Mrs. Strathern said.

"Well…it's a committee of one if you'll take it on again."

The other woman nodded.

"I'll help. And so will Mona. Give her something to do," Mrs. Strathern said, always looking for a way to distract her boy-crazy daughter into some productive activity.

"Entertainment?" Mrs. Proctor prompted. "Oh, that was Glenda last year."

"I'll bring her excellent Victrola and records," I said on her behalf, sure that she would attend the event. If not, I would do the honors with the machine from her house.

"Mr. Olsen has agreed to provide the tables, some of them might need to come from the school. You'll take care of that, won't you?" Mrs. Proctor said, looking to Miss Olsen at her side.

"Your father can round up some young men to set them up the night before. Now, let's see…we'll keep the same judging categories as last year."

"As always," someone added.

"Do we want to have a raffle?" Miss Ballantine asked, then put her hand over her mouth for speaking, knowing that the task would fall to her.

"Excellent suggestion! Just find about three or four businesses here or in Adams that are willing to provide something or some service." Mrs. Proctor looked down at her list, and Miss Ballantine wondered what she had got herself into.

"Everyone knows that the proceeds from the Garden Fair will go to the restoration fund for the church, so I came up with a rather clever idea, if I don't say so myself. I talked to the owner of the garden center in Adams, who agreed to sell some plants, implements and ceramic pots. After all, who attends a garden event who doesn't garden? He has agreed to give us a portion of the sales," Mrs. Proctor said.

"Well done," Miss Manley said. "You are enterprising!"

"We usually have people from Adams come over, but I thought I would get some flyers printed up and circulate them there to make sure we have a good turnout," Miss Olsen said.

"You might want to let the Fosters at the Mountain Aire Hotel know about the event, too," I said. "People from out of town may want to do something different on a weekend. I'll be happy to take some flyers over for you."

Mrs. Proctor beamed at me. "Miss Burnside, as a relative newcomer to our fair town, I also thought it might be a good idea for you to be one of the judges."

I stammered before saying, "I'm afraid I know very little about what constitutes the best petunia or the perfect tomato."

"Exactly! We want someone to look at this with fresh eyes. And you have the credentials of coming from New York City. There will be three judges, Reverend Lewis, yourself and," she paused shuffling through her papers.

"One of the County Commissioners!" Miss Tierney said, to the approval of all of the group save one. Mrs. Proctor scowled at the suggestion and her friend immediately said, "Sorry," knowing that Mrs. Proctor had declared her candidacy for the County Commissioner election in November and did not intend for one of her opponents to get more notoriety than she.

There were glances around the room at the faux pas, but Mrs. Proctor picked up the pace immediately and said, "The Postmaster!" She then waved a sheet of paper in front of her face. "Here is the sign-up sheet for refreshments. Since this is a charitable event, I think it is entirely appropriate that we charge for the drinks and the food."

By the reaction from the group, this must have been a new idea, but it was a smart one—if they had a captive audience and wanted to make some money. I was getting into the spirit of the event.

"Mrs. Proctor, you have such wonderful organizational skills!" Mrs. Rockmore observed.

"Well, I was President of my sorority at Middlebury," she said. "I majored en Français!"

Most of the group was as impressed as was I since college had not been an option for me, but I also detected an undercurrent of annoyance from those who had heard this boast more than once.

"Have I left anything out?" Mrs. Proctor asked, adjusting her glasses.

"Do we have anything for the little children?" Nina Lewis asked before closing her eyes as she knew what was coming next.

"What a wonderful idea! Were you thinking of a petting zoo? Or a donkey ride?" Mrs. Proctor asked.

"Heavens, no! I was thinking of a fenced-off corral and a volunteer teenager who could look after a few of the little ones."

Mrs. Proctor was disappointed by the backpedaling but pushed on. "You think what is best, Mrs. Lewis. Let me know what you come up with." She took a sip of her tea, and the committee assignment portion of the tea group was apparently at an end.

"Don't forget! My campaign committee meeting is tomorrow at the library," she added.

I didn't know exactly what the County Commissioners did for the folks of Berkshire County, but based upon Mrs. Proctor's performance that afternoon, it was clear she could summon resources, recruit labor and command other people effortlessly.

Chapter 3

A bit of a surprise the next morning was the appearance of Farley Dexter at the Adams office since we had assumed he had left the area completely. He looked much the same as he had in early spring: long billowing cloak, long hair and the preposterous neck scarf in what was warm weather for these parts. I thought back to the vision of him seated in front of the fireplace at the Old Welby farm he had bought, burning paper to keep himself warm in the drafty house. Even though it was early summer in town, out on the distant farms, the buildings were probably cold inside if that is where he was still living.

He nodded in my direction with little emotion, likely still angry at everyone involved in bringing down his mushroom-growing enterprise, which included John and me.

"Mr. Dexter," I said by way of greeting.

"I was wondering if the doctor were in?" he asked.

"Do you have an appointment?" I asked, consulting the book but knowing he hadn't one.

"No," he sighed. He sat down in the reception room anyway and looked at me in expectation.

"I'll see if he's busy," I said, getting up.

I went into John's office, closing the door behind me. "Farley Dexter is here and would like to talk to you."

He made an exasperated face but got up, nonetheless, since the man was usually there for a chat rather than a medical issue.

"Yes, Mr. Dexter, may I help you?" John asked, putting his hands in the pockets of his white coat.

Our visitor seemed at a loss for words.

"Medical or social visit?" John asked with a smile.

He latched onto the lifeline. "Medical."

"Very well, step this way. Surely you want to hang up your cloak?"

As Dexter did so, John turned to me. "Nurse?" and I followed him into the examination room and began to potter around with the instruments and straighten out the jars and bottles on the countertop. I smiled to myself, knowing that my assistance was not needed; John just wanted me to observe what might be another strange encounter.

"What seems to be the matter?"

"I have a bit of a rash," he said, rolling the filthy cuffs of his shirt up to the elbows on both arms. "See?"

I glanced and indeed noticed red splotches from his wrists to the crook of his arm.

"Have you been touching anything out of the ordinary? Plants of any kind?"

"No."

"Clearing brush or nettles from the property?"

"No," he answered with a scoff.

I could hardly imagine him involved in any form of manual labor. Even though the mushroom farm was technically defunct, he might still have some workers there to do the heavy lifting.

John took a magnifying glass from a drawer and examined the man's skin more carefully. "Is this the only place you have this rash?"

"Yes."

"It doesn't look like poison ivy. Are you using some kind of harsh soap on your skin or clothing?"

Dexter thought for a moment. Without his odd cloak and with a decent haircut, he could appear to be a regular fellow, even a handsome one. His hygiene left something to be desired, judging by the dirty shirt, and I wondered if the application of soap and water alone might cure what ailed him.

"Dermatitis is what we call it, meaning irritation of the skin. That doesn't give us the cause, however. Have you got an adequate change of clothes up at the farm?"

This seemed a perplexing question. "Um, I have a few shirts."

"What I'm asking is: are they adequately washed and rinsed thoroughly before you wear them?"

"I don't know. Someone else does the laundry. One of the men."

"There might be something in the laundry soap or the well water itself that is irritating your skin. I would suggest that you bring your clothes into town to the laundry and have them professionally washed. That could be the source. In the meantime, let's apply some calming lotion and see if that helps."

And get out of that disgusting shirt, I thought.

I got a basin and filled it with water and witch hazel and swabbed his arms. Each gauze pad came away a little less dirty and I couldn't help but think that a good bath would do a world of good.

John was busy prescribing some cream while informing the patient that the pharmacist would have it on hand.

"Maybe I should stay in town for a few days," Dexter said.

His financial situation baffled me. He seemed to be able to afford to stay at a hotel, yet chose to live up at the farm. He had a gaggle of wealthy friends in New York who were going to be investors in what he had dubbed his health farm, although they hadn't come through with the funding as far as anyone knew. After the incident in April, they had quickly scattered back to the City and hadn't been seen since.

"Have you seen Doctor Bentley lately?" John inquired, referring to Dexter's friend.

"No. I don't know where he and his wife went, but he left me with the mess at the farm to clean up. Maybe this is a nervous reaction to all the difficulties I've had to face."

"That's possible."

"You know that the County wants me to fill in those trenches and tunnels and the ninety days they gave me to do so are almost up. Mr. King came personally up to the farm although the County has employees who had already reported the situation to him. He was very nasty about it, too, suggesting that the farm and all who lived on it were a blight to the community. I don't know how I can clean anything up without heavy equipment that I don't have. There are two men up there and they can't be expected to do it all by themselves with shovels and wheelbarrows. I don't even know if I have any wheelbarrows."

"What happens next?" John asked.

"I suppose they will condemn the property. I've tried to talk to the other Commissioners about it, but they are not interested in my explanation and defer to Mr. King. Most of the tunnels were dug by the farmer who owned the place before me, so I shouldn't be responsible for fixing it."

According to what Officer Reed had said to us earlier, much of the digging seemed to have been done on Dexter's watch, but he could plead ignorance.

"It wasn't until after I bought it that I discovered the root cellar and the extensions that he had made underground. Maybe I could just roll big rocks in front of the entrances or iron gates like they do for abandoned mines out west." He looked up hopefully for reassurance that it was a good idea.

John shrugged. "It might be better to talk to the County officials again and see what your options are."

"Mr. King also suggested that they could condemn the house, too. The whole situation is incredibly unfair." Dexter rolled down his sleeves and seemed to consider his options. "Thank you, Doctor."

"Will you be staying at the Adams Hotel or back at the farm?" I asked conversationally, although I intended to find out where to send the bill.

"I guess I'll be at the hotel. Maybe buy some shirts as long as I'm in town," he muttered before shuffling out of the exam room to get his cloak and leave in a dejected fashion.

―――

WE DROVE BACK to West Adams, John to fix himself a sandwich and I to Miss Manley's for a hot lunch that Annie had prepared. I realized I was spoiled by getting three meals a day, a large bedroom overlooking the forest behind the garden and good conversation during our meals. We had just finished when the telephone rang, and Annie summoned me to take a call from Glenda.

"You'll never guess!" she said. That's usually how she began a conversation. And of course, I never could guess. "We're coming home this weekend."

It stumped me for a moment because I now thought of Manhattan as her home, but she meant the house next door in West Adams.

"That's lovely. Just for the weekend?"

"No, that's the wonderful part. Douglas and I will there the entire summer. I can't wait to leave the City."

"But you were so entranced with living there. And what about your new apartment?"

"I loved living here as a single girl, not a young mother with a very big baby to lug up and down stairs and in and out of buildings. Our new apartment is swell, but I'll be away from it for a few months. When we go back at the end of the summer, I'll tackle the decorating then."

"What about the Nelsons? Are you expecting them to move out?" I thought about the mother, daughter and granddaughter displaced once again.

"It's in the works. Elsie will be leaving the Lewises soon, when she and Sam get married, and I've talked to Nina already and she's prepared to take on Joanna and the baby."

I was trying to work out how the household would be organized but remembered that the parsonage had four bedrooms, enough to accommodate Reverend Lewis and Nina, their nephew Roger, who would be going off to college in the fall, Joanna and now two babies in the nursery. Things would be noisy and complicated.

"What about Mrs. Nelson?"

"She can stay here. After all, we've got two girls coming up soon to do the writing."

My head was swimming with all the changes. "What two girls? Writing what?"

"Oh, Aggie, if I weren't so lazy, I would have written you all about it. The books that Stuart wrote got redone for a younger audience and they've become popular. They're gobbling them up. These two gals are working with the company to pump out more stories to the series. He gives them the outline and theme and they crank out the dialogue and action sequences. They are quite clever and work very fast."

Beyond anyone's wildest expectations, Stuart's publishing venture was thriving. Miss Manley would be pleased, but I would leave it to Glenda to share the news herself when she got here.

"I'm glad Stuart has done so well."

"He is clever. Not only has he got Cash Ridley as an investor, but he's also made money on the side. The girls will be renting from us with the expenses charged off to the company. Isn't that brilliant?"

It was. I wasn't sure whether his partners knew about the deal or if it was even legal, but that wasn't my business.

"Oops, I hear Douglas. I've got to go." She hung up quickly.

I returned to the dining room to see Miss Manley looking at me with curiosity.

"That was Glenda. They're coming up this weekend and there are so many other changes and arrangements to tell you about, but I have to get to work."

"I hope they are good changes."

"There're going to be a lot of babies around this summer," I said.

Naturally, I shared the news with John, who was trying to understand the complicated shifting of households but was more interested in Stuart's venture.

"It appears he has made something of himself. At last."

"Now, John." He was not the biggest fan of Stuart Manley, whom he considered too puffed up for his own good. I shared his opinion but didn't voice it, especially since I suspected that his aunt financed a good deal of his ventures. Or at least came to the rescue when things hadn't worked out in the past. Now, I began to wonder if they had simply changed apartments or bought one that was a different kettle of fish altogether. Just months ago, they were scrambling for cash and anxious to rent the West Adams house. Well, they had tenants now. And a live-in maid/cook/nanny for Douglas to boot.

We had a busy afternoon of drop-in patients with minor ailments, and with a busy reception room, they all felt a need to chat with me. I shared the news about Glenda's coming up that weekend and so many were pleased to know that she would be spending the summer with her young son. I had forgotten that the people in a small town such as West Adams always cared for their own and she would likely get a lot of support and attention, something that had been sorely lacking in New York.

The telephone was busy, too, and I was surprised that one of the calls was for me. It was Mrs. Proctor, who wanted to make sure that I would attend her campaign meeting after work. She was canny; I was certain that I hadn't volunteered to assist her. And I wondered how it would look to John if I was to be actively engaged in unseating Mr. King or one of the other County Commissioners, however that worked.

"Mrs. Proctor, I'm sorry, but I have a busy work schedule and don't think I could…."

"Miss Burnside, your opinion is very valuable to me. You've spent your life in the big city and know infinitely more than I or any of my supporters about big city politics."

What was she talking about? "How nice of you to say that, but I haven't had any involvement with political life except to vote when I came of age."

"But still, you have your finger on the pulse of life in our town and have been in touch with so many people in the county. I know you can add so much to our knowledge. We'll be expecting you at the library at six-thirty. Goodbye."

I stared at the telephone. What to do? I didn't want to offend her and certainly didn't want to put the kibosh on John's loan application from Mr. King, the incumbent whose position she challenged. I decided that I would attend this one meeting with the explicit understanding that I was there as a guest and could not participate further. She was a formidable woman who would try to inveigle me into canvassing or writing support letters, but I was going to hold strong and not commit to anything further. So I thought.

Chapter 4

I felt I had to tell John about Mrs. Proctor's intentions and he was surprisingly blasé about the idea.

"She knows a lot of people. I don't see anything wrong with it. But you do have a full-time job, unlike some of her other supporters who can stuff envelopes or make visits to potential voters—however that works."

"She seems to think that, because I lived near the City, I somehow absorbed the machinations of Tammany Hall."

That got a laugh from him.

"You could be a ward healer!" he said. "Just think of the power you could wield if Mrs. Proctor wins. Which she won't, of course, because voters don't vote for female candidates."

He turned back to his paperwork.

"There have been women elected to office," I said stoutly.

"Yes, but they were often the widows of men who died in office."

"Not always," I said. I wracked my brain to think of examples. I would just go to the library early and do a little research, but I had the sinking feeling that he could be right.

I let Miss Manley know I would be a bit late for dinner, changed my clothes and made my way to the tiny library adjacent to the town hall. The librarian, a woman who volunteered her time three afternoons a week, was still there, probably to let the campaign committee in, and I asked her for some help in my research.

"Oh, my, that is a difficult topic. You might have to look in the encyclopedia by country or by state. That would take a long time. But let's put our heads together for a moment and think."

Her head was considerably older and grayer than mine, so I anticipated a fount of knowledge and was not disappointed.

"Queen Victoria comes to mind, but, of course, she was neither American nor elected. Hmm." She twisted her mouth and went to the volumes of the encyclopedia that some generous patron had donated.

"I know there were women elected to Congress, but I just have to find the right reference." She picked up one volume, then another, and leafed through them, not satisfied with the results. "There is a list of members of Congress in each session and, maybe if we look at the list, we can ascertain how many women there were. We'll get thrown off by some names, like Leslie, which is often a man's name, but let's give it a try."

She was animated by the search and took a sheet of paper and pencil and read out the names while I looked over her shoulder and copied them down. It was a surprising list. Of course, it was Congress, not the Berkshire County Commissioners, and the information was from 1930, but it bolstered my feelings of under-representation. If I could not supply the political savvy Mrs. Proctor looked for, I could at least show her the list of women who had been elected to the Congress of the United States. It didn't seem that I could find what I was looking for in this small library, but perhaps a trip to Pittsfield could tell me if most of them won on their merit, not inheriting the seat from a deceased spouse.

Mrs. Proctor came bustling in with Miss Olsen in tow, carrying papers and what appeared to be a rolled-up map.

"My, you're the early bird!" she exclaimed. I was always impressed by her energy and her tidy appearance. Neat as a pin, as my mother would say.

She nodded to the librarian and began to arrange the papers on the one table in the room.

"I think we have enough chairs," she said, putting her hand to her chin. I saw the thin gold wedding band and tried to remember what Mr. Proctor looked like, also what it must be like to be married to such a formidable woman.

Miss Olsen rolled out the map and secured it with her handbag at one edge while the librarian generously provided three small volumes to hold down the other corners. It was a map of Berkshire County and it looked like Mrs. Proctor or her protegee had done her homework, outlining in the red the electoral districts for County Commissioner. I looked it over, recognizing the names of the small towns, many of which I had not yet visited. There were other place names on the map alongside marked roads I had traveled but I didn't remember seeing any houses or inhabitants.

"I've been past there," I pointed, "but is the town hidden from the road?"

"No, that's named after an early settler. The house and barn were gone long before I was born, but people still call the area by his name."

I thought that was odd but perhaps handy in giving directions to someone. But what good would it do for a stranger if there was no marker or sign?

The door opened and Miss Tierney and Mrs. Rockmore came in and were welcomed warmly.

"Isn't Mrs. Lewis coming?" Miss Olsen asked.

"The baby," I answered with a knowing look. It was a good excuse she had provided me, but the reality is she didn't want to get pulled into politics.

"Of course," she murmured and smoothed out the map.

"Well, then let's begin," Mrs. Proctor said. She looked over at the librarian, who decided to busy herself with some paperwork. She had to stay until the end of the meeting to lock up but probably didn't want to get involved with the campaign committee and made herself invisible.

"I'm so delighted you have agreed to assist me in this historic endeavor. I want to begin by reminding you that a political campaign runs on strategy and tactics. You mustn't share any of the information we discuss, even with your nearest and dearest. I intend to run a tight ship."

I didn't doubt it and the not-so-subtle look in the librarian's direction told me that she would not tolerate a spy, either.

"Miss Olsen was kind enough to find a map and provide us with some perspective. Now, most of you know there are three Commissioners, each with a district. We are in District 1, the northern part of the county, District 2 is Pittsfield and District 3 is the southern area. I will be challenging Mr. King in District 1."

"Who are the other two?" I asked.

"District 2 is Mr. Headley. You've heard of the Headley paper company, I imagine," she said. "One of the largest employers in the area and a guaranteed voter base for him."

There were murmurs of disapproval.

"A rather young man for the job with a roving eye," Mrs. Rockmore added with a derisive sniff.

More murmurs.

"Mr. Campbell has District 3. As did his father and his uncle before him. They own the lumber mill."

A knowing smile flickered across Miss Tierney's mouth.

A banker, a factory owner and a hereditary position sounded like an impregnable bunch to me, especially if they banded together to hold on to their positions.

"Now, why, you may ask, do I wish to take on Mr. King? I will tell you why in one word. Cronyism. These three men decide among themselves who will get what piece of the county pie. We all pay taxes and what do we see in exchange for them? There has been no road work in our district in years."

"But the Depression," Miss Tierney began.

"Bosh! Our taxes have not gone down since the Crash. No millionaires are living here who have lost their fortunes."

For a moment, I thought about the mansions that Stuart Manley had shown me one day when he took Glenda and me for a tour of historic homes in the area. I wondered if their owners had suffered as a result of the economic downturn.

"The bridge that goes up past the Ross property is in danger of falling and all those men talk about is buying heavy equipment. Toys for boys! It's too much 'I'll scratch your back if you scratch mine' going on. And Pittsfield gets the lion's share of the projects."

"They do have more people living there," Miss Tierney said.

Mrs. Rockmore gave her a withering glance that was tempered by a smile. "My dear, the districts are based on population. So even though there appear to be more people in Pittsfield, they are clumped in one location. The folks in our district are spread out all over in small towns and farms. There is no reason why the funding can't be equitable."

"Why hasn't Mr. King represented us better, then?" Miss Tierney persisted.

"Indeed. Would anyone venture a guess?"

"Because he is a banker," I said before thinking.

Mrs. Proctor pointed at me. "Exactly! What do bankers do but make friends with important men who will bring business to their bank? And to whom do the bankers make their loans? The very same people. As long as we have a banker with the interest of his bank, his job, his salary and the backers as the most important thing on his mind, we'll be left with decrepit bridges and roads that are falling apart."

Mrs. Rockmore clapped loudly. "That's a wonderful speech! I hope you'll use it."

Mrs. Proctor shook her head. "No, I do not intend to smear him personally. Unless I need to. But I will point out that we do not get our share of the county's resources for our needs."

"It's only fair to share," I said.

"My word, Miss Burnside! I knew you would be an asset to the campaign. That's the slogan! 'It's only fair to share!'" She smiled broadly and I had a sinking feeling I was being sucked into something I needed no part of.

I held my hands out to pause the excitement. "Mrs. Proctor, please. I cannot be part of your campaign committee. I only agreed to attend because…you asked for my opinion." *Why did I agree to attend? Was it pride?* "My work for Doctor Taylor comes first and I can't alienate patients because of political issues."

She twisted her mouth in concentration. "I understand perfectly. But that doesn't mean that I can't pick your mind for how things are done in the City."

I don't know what she thought was in my political mind, but it wasn't anything about campaigns.

"For instance, how do candidates know what their constituents want?"

That seemed obvious to me. "If they are already elected, they have heard from them. If they haven't been elected yet, they go to picnics and other group meetings—by invitation, usually—and introduce themselves. Sometimes they hold a meeting or rally somewhere public and let folks know about it beforehand and make a speech."

"Miss Olsen, are you writing this down?" Mrs. Proctor said.

"They also go door to door and introduce themselves to the voters and ask what is on their minds. If there is a lot of ground to cover, they enlist volunteers to help them. And have them take notes as they go along, of course. Not just on the issues but on whether the voter is a likely supporter or not."

"Our district is large but among all of us and our friends, we know a lot of people."

"In the City, the campaigns that are well funded have little cards or flyers printed up. You know, 'Vote for Me' kind of thing. And what I have seen is that there is some information about what the candidate promises to do. We used to get them all the time in the mail. Or hand-delivered to our house."

Mrs. Proctor's eyes were glowing, and I thought she might be about to cry. But as I came to know her better, that was not a likely response.

"Miss Burnside. You have given me so many ideas! How can I ever thank you?"

The assembled women clapped in unison, and I felt myself blush.

"You're welcome. But please, leave my name out of it. I don't think it would be good for Doctor Taylor's practice to appear partisan." Nor would it be a good idea to cross Mr. King with a business loan in the making.

Chapter 5

Friday afternoon brought Stuart and Glenda to town with Douglas in a cot in the back seat of the yellow Packard. What once seemed to be the eligible bachelor's vehicle was now loaded down with suitcases and baby gear. Both parents looked weary from the long trip, but their son was gurgling away, kicking his legs and stuffing something in his mouth.

Miss Manley and Annie dashed out to the driveway next door to admire the baby while I tagged behind.

"He's adorable," Annie said. "And so big!"

Glenda hugged Annie. "You can't believe how something that small can eat so much."

"Is he taking solid food yet?" Annie, the eldest of her siblings, was well aware of the developmental milestones.

"Rice cereal and formula mostly to tide him over until the morning."

"He's precious," Miss Manley said, clasping her hands in front of her in admiration. "And he does look like Daddy," she smiled at her nephew, whose hair was a bit on end, either from the open window of the car or raking it with his hands.

He embraced his aunt warmly. "What a trip! The young man wanted to sit in his mother's lap the whole way, yanking on her hair and trying to chew her necklace. He made a right fuss when we put him in the cot for a nap."

"Let me hold him," Miss Manley said. I often wondered about her life as a spinster, which is what people called unmarried women of her age. Did she miss the company of family, of a husband or children? She was usually busy knitting something for a friend's child or grandchild and I hoped that people would always remember her kindness.

"Oh, he is rather large," she said, bending to pick him up as he stared at her wide-eyed.

"Be careful, there are days when my back aches from all the lifting. I can't wait until he starts to walk."

"That's when the trouble begins," Annie said.

"The house and yard look fine, thank goodness," Glenda said. "Let's see what the inside is like. Maybe it's overrun with raccoons, mushrooms and vines."

"Sam was good enough to mow the lawn and check the inside to see that all was in working order and I gave it a good once-over," Annie said. "And the Nelsons are very tidy women."

"Thank you.."

We all helped them unload the car and hump the suitcases up the stairs.

"Where are the two young women who are working for you?"

"We couldn't fit the Crompton sisters in the car with all the paraphernalia Douglas requires. They're coming up by bus tomorrow and Stuart will pick them up in Pittsfield. They've lived in the City all their lives, so this should be an interesting change for them," Glenda said. "We'll put them in the back bedroom."

"How long will they stay?" I asked.

"For the summer. You'd be surprised at how quickly they work. They can almost read each other's minds, or at least finish each other's sentences most of the time. I can't wait to see Nina's little girl," Glenda said, looking toward the Lewises' house.

"I'm sure you'll be seeing quite a lot of each other. Her name is Eleanor, and she is a miniature of her mother. And dressed to the nines at all times, as well," I said.

"I would expect nothing less. Let's get settled and we'll meet you in the garden for cocktails," Glenda said with a wink. Just like old times.

Sometime later, we were a merry group seated in chairs under the trees.

"A bootleg bottle of gin, a bowl of ice and thou," Stuart intoned to his wife, who smiled back at him and their son, sitting upon a blanket, the center of attention.

"Just look at those chubby legs," Glenda said proudly. "Where's Nina? I'm dying to see her little girl."

"There is some sort of church function just now, but maybe Joanna can bring her over along with Rosalie, her little girl."

"How can she manage with two babies?" Stuart asked.

"Strong arms, I guess," I said.

"That's me, all right," said John, carrying the Lewises' little girl, who looked even smaller than usual in his large embrace. "Joanna's on her way." He put his charge carefully on the blanket on her stomach as she was still a bit too young to sit up properly. The two babies observed each other.

"Don't you sometimes wonder what's going on in their little heads?" Glenda asked, sipping her drink.

"'When's dinner' is what he's thinking." At Stuart's laughter at his joke, Douglas turned to smile at him. "Isn't he a charmer?"

"Dinner will be very soon. Annie has made a feast for us all but after tonight, you're on your own," Miss Manley reminded them.

"We know. Mrs. Nelson has gone into town, and her hard work will start tomorrow after I pick up the Cromptons."

John reached his hand out for a drink and looked puzzled.

"They're busy bees who type like maniacs and giggle at each other's jokes."

"You'll have a lively household," he said.

"I'm so looking forward to some company. Adult company, that is," Glenda said, leaning back in the chair and imagining a summer of leisure ahead.

Things got complicated quickly after Stuart brought the sisters back to West Adams the next day. The sisters were 'two peas in a pod,' as my mother would say, both of average height, full-busted with tiny waists, cute button noses and shiny, wavy, chestnut-colored hair. With the improbable names of Minerva and Freya, no less. They chattered incessantly in a good-hearted manner, but for Glenda, who had been used to tending to her son for long periods on her own, I could tell that the sudden company of so many people was jarring. Stuart went to play a game of tennis with Roger, while the young women settled in, commenting on the house, the baby, the pictures on the wall in a constant stream of speech. I was only present for the first hour of their visit and even I found it a bit exhausting. They were soon lugging portable typewriters into the room.

"Where shall we set up?" they asked Mrs. Nelson, who deferred to Glenda.

As usual, Glenda hadn't mentally prepared herself for what the arrangements would be. They couldn't work in their bedroom; it was too small and the baby's room was next door, which would be too much noise for him. The sitting room was available but then the family couldn't use it during the day. They settled on the dining room which, outside of mealtime, could accommodate the two portable typewriters and the paperwork. It still meant a lot of adjustment and moving of things, but it would have to work.

Stuart got back from tennis and had a meeting with the Cromptons for about an hour while Glenda and I wheeled Douglas into town in the baby carriage that Annie had lent her. He sat up and took in the sights and the admiration of those in town on a Saturday afternoon.

"It's so good to be back," Glenda said.

I think she envisioned a long, peaceful holiday but it turned out to be anything but that. Dinner was a handful for Mrs. Nelson, cooking for four adults and unused to the lively conversation at the table. Douglas was propped in a highchair on loan from Annie's family, banging a spoon on the tray and smiling in delight at the noise he made.

"I don't remember it being quite so raucous growing up," Glenda said.

"You were the only child, remember. If anyone was making a racket, it would have been you," her husband said.

She was a bit down in the mouth because Stuart had to leave on Sunday, and she was still unsure of Mrs. Nelson's capabilities. Glenda came over to Miss Manley's after dinner and asked me whether the woman could cook, clean and take care of Douglas.

"Obviously, not at the same time," I said. If she had images of the two of us gallivanting around while others did all the work, she had another thing coming. I had a full-time job, the weekend was almost over and Mrs. Nelson had her hands full with cooking and cleaning. What spare time she had was to be devoted to seeing her granddaughter, Rosalie, and helping Joanna get accustomed to motherhood and her job duties. It was going to be a complicated balancing act for all the women.

The relative quiet of Glenda's weekend was shattered Monday morning with the clacking of the typewriters—two of them—interrupted by the ding as the margin approached and the slamming of the carriage back for the next line. I could even hear it in Miss Manley's dining room as we finished breakfast.

"Oh, dear. It sounds like a factory," she said.

Minutes later, Glenda appeared with Douglas in her arms. "I'm going to go positively insane from that racket. They pound away on those keys as they mean it!"

"I should hope so," I said, glad that we were one house away.

"They do sound productive," Miss Manley said mildly.

"Consider it the sound of money being made," I suggested as I got up to put my dishes in the kitchen.

"Where are you going?" Glenda asked.

"To work, silly."

"All day?"

"That's what full-time means. You know we're over in Adams in the morning and back here for the afternoon."

"Will I see you for lunch?"

"If you like." I couldn't understand why she was acting so needy. "As long as we don't get held up with a patient in Adams. Why don't you make a habit of taking Douglas for a stroll each day? He'll enjoy the fresh air, as will you, and all the neighbor ladies can 'ooh' and 'ahh' over how cute he is."

She nodded, looking a bit morose. "Maybe I'll take him over to Nina's and the babies can play."

They were too young to play with each other, but it would give the mothers some time to chat and Joanna a break from her work.

By the time I returned for lunch, the machine noise was more muffled and Miss Manley explained why. Glenda had the wonderful idea to set the Crompton sisters up in the shed behind the Lewises' house that once housed an artist's studio. With two card tables in place and the plentiful northern light coming in, the separate structure allowed them to fully focus on their work and gave Glenda her dining room and quiet back. She was pleased with her solution and popped in to see me and crow about how she and Douglas would be able to nap in peace. As we chatted, we could hear the rat-a-tat of the typewriter keys come to a halt and then laughter.

Glenda put her head to one side, rather in the same fashion that Miss Manley had when considering a problem. "That's odd."

"Are they breaking for lunch?"

More laughter.

She handed the baby to me and went out the sitting room door toward the shed next door. I plopped Douglas on Miss Manley's lap and followed; curiosity always gets the better of me.

Glenda knocked gently on the door and stepped in to see the sisters seated at their tables, smoke rising in the air from their cigarettes while Roger stood nearby.

"Hullo," he said cheerfully to Glenda. "I was just entertaining the Crumpets."

They thought their new nickname was very funny and laughed along with him.

"He's promised to take us to play tennis at the Mountain Aire Hotel," Freya said.

"Yes, I got my old job back. One of the perks is being able to bring guests up for a game. There's a swimming pool, too," he added.

They practically swooned at the notion of a pool and turning, they noticed me outside the door in my uniform.

"Oh, I didn't realize you were a nurse," Minerva said.

"I don't wear it on the weekend after all. But I worked hard for the privilege of wearing it and wear it I shall."

"Oh, Min," said Freya. "She could be a character in the next book, when they go on that luxury cruise."

I was startled at the thought.

They both laughed. "We don't use people's real names, of course. Although we may borrow a bit of what you look like." They took a good long look at me and I felt unclothed. "Don't worry, unless you mind being described as a tall, attractive and competent woman."

"I'll go for that," I said.

"Come on, you two, time for lunch. Where's the baby?" Glenda asked.

"Who?" I teased her.

"You're supposed to put little bells on his shoes to tell where he wanders off to," Freya said.

"He can't walk yet. Thank goodness."

We all trooped out of the little shed back to our respective houses, which made me wonder aloud what Roger was doing home in the middle of the day.

"Teachers are prepping for our exams, so we have the afternoon off. Just think, in another few months, I won't be having to go to classes from nine to three each day."

He would be attending Williams College, not far away, a prestigious accomplishment for someone I had thought was not a serious student. But if he thought once he was accepted the hard work was over, he likely had a big surprise coming. Graduates of his high school attended Williams and had filled his head with stories of hijinks, parties and fraternity associations that were paramount at the time. I could tell by Reverend Lewis's strained expressions when Roger was around that he was already worried about the social influence the young man might be under.

"Lots of changes in store for everyone," I said to Annie as I went through the kitchen.

She looked puzzled as I walked by, wondering what to expect next.

The sisters broke off from their typing in the late afternoon and came over to John's office with Glenda to be introduced. I overheard their conversation as they approached the door.

"Is he the dreamy doctor?"

"He's taken," said Glenda to my relief and amusement.

They entered, all excitement and chatter, bantering with one another and looking around the office with curiosity.

"This would do quite nicely," Freya said.

"For what?" John asked.

"We get handed the general plot and characters but are expected to come up with dialogue and descriptions of the locale. So, it's good to be out of the City—"

"And out into some fresh air and scenery—"

"And get a look at different rooms, houses, accents, faces, professions, scenery."

"This is all going to be such a good experience for us."

"Min, I'm going to use this layout for the infirmary on the boat. Only smaller, of course."

They continued talking to each other, almost forgetting we were there, until Glenda suggested that we all have a small cocktail before dinner. That turned the conversational level up a notch and it seemed that West Adams wasn't going to be the end of the earth for them, after all.

"Roger has invited us to the Mountain Aire Hotel for tennis and a swim sometime. What else is there to do around here?" Freya asked.

We looked at one another, struggling to come up with something that might be as exciting as the offerings in Manhattan like the theater, museums or restaurants.

"There is a very harmonious choir at the church on Sunday," Glenda said.

"So many outdoor activities. Hiking, walking, bird watching…." I trailed off.

"Do you like to fish or hunt?" John asked to their wide-eyed faces.

"I like to swim, but we've never gone fishing."

"That might be something to do, don't you think, ladies?" John asked.

"The Garden Fair is coming up very soon," I added. "Exhibitions of plants, vegetables and flowers that folks have grown."

"Baked goods and canned goods competition," Glenda said.

"Pony rides for the children."

"Will there be a merry-go-round or a Ferris wheel? I love those," Minerva asked.

"I don't think so. This is more of a rural community."

The sisters whispered to each other and then turned to us. "We could supply the fortune teller and assistant. It's a fun parlor game kind of thing we've done back home. Very silly, lots of fun," Freya said.

"I vill tell your fortune," Minerva said in an exaggerated accent and a deepened voice. "Gif me your hand." They both laughed. "But we don't have our costumes and didn't bring many changes of clothes."

"Don't worry. I've got an attic full of stuff. I know my mother had this frilly white blouse that would be perfect. And she had a lot of scarves that you could put to use."

"That would be marvelous," Freya said.

Glenda brightened up. "Now that you mention it, we should look for some other entertainment. Somebody must know magic tricks. Or how about a singer?"

"Dancers?" I suggested.

"I could do the snake charming bit," John said, and we stared at him. "With a fake snake, of course."

"You have a phony snake in your house somewhere?"

"Yes, I won it at a carnival."

"That's an idea. Let's get a few games set up, too. Toss the beanbag, fish for pennies with a magnet on a string, knock down the stacked-up cans and a sack race. Let's get together tonight after dinner and brainstorm more ideas. Oh, this will be a much better Garden Fair than the staid juiciest tomato competition," Glenda said. "Won't Mrs. Proctor be pleased that we have come up with some interesting entertainment other than a Victrola playing?"

I thought it was a capital idea to have something for people to do besides admiring potted plants and flowers in vases. But I wasn't so sure that Mrs. Proctor would like her thunder stolen.

We did meet after dinner in the cool of the yard, and although it was still light, we had turned the back porch light on. Glenda begged off reluctantly, needing to tend to Douglas. The Crompton sisters were brimming with energy, ideas and high spirits as we talked about what might be fun for such an event.

"Do we need a small stage of some kind? You know, so that announcements can be made and any performers could be seen."

"That's an idea, Min. Get the word around town that the Garden Fair is looking for entertainment! There must be people who would sing."

"Or play the spoons?" Minerva asked. I didn't know if I had ever experienced that, but it was a possibility.

"Maybe there are some children who play an instrument. Not a piano, of course. We couldn't haul one out onto the grass. This is an outdoor event, isn't it?" Freya asked.

"Yes, adjacent to the church in that grassy area. I don't think you've seen it yet. Although the church has an organ and, if the doors were left open, you'd be able to hear it outside."

"Not church music?" Freya asked. "That would be too somber."

"You can play the Charleston on the organ," Minerva said, and we all laughed at the notion.

John walked up at that moment, hiding something behind his back. "Well, here is Moe."

He pulled out a four-foot-long, garish green snake made out of some toweling material. It had a red forked tongue hanging from its mouth and large googly eyes.

"And what does Moe do?" I asked.

"Observe," he said. He slipped one hand underneath its head and supported the body with the opposite arm and addressed it. "Well, Moe, how have things been?"

"A bit dusty up in the attic," was the answer in a falsetto voice that John managed.

We clapped and laughed.

"Where were you before that?" Minerva asked.

"Oh, here and there. Carnival life was a bit exhausting until this guy brought me home."

I don't know which was funnier, the silly voice that John had created for the snake, his total lack of expertise as a ventriloquist, or the notion that he would consider performing.

"You know what would be hysterical, Aggie? If you were to appear in your nurse's outfit and pretend the snake was a patient. Oh, Doctor, even better, if you wear your white coat and take his temperature and so on."

He thought it was a great idea, as did I, and we promised to work out some dialogue of questions and answers, although just the notion of the town doctor making a stuffed snake talk would be amusing enough. We kept laughing at the thought of the children who would get a kick out of it and only stopped when we heard footsteps along the back path. It was getting to be dusk and difficult to make out more than a man's shape emerging from the shadows of the trees.

"Hello, I didn't mean to disturb your party. I was looking for Reverend Lewis's house and someone directed me along this path."

"You're almost there," I said. "It's just next door. They should have told you how to go the front way." As I said this, I realized he must not be a local person who would have been familiar with the shortcuts.

He stepped forward into the light from the porch and I heard the Crompton sisters gasp. There stood the most handsome man I had ever seen. Tall, with broad shoulders yet an athletic build, blond hair swept back, deep-set eyes and the most engaging smile anyone could produce on a first meeting. He focused on the Cromptons, who returned his smile.

"Goodness, this seems like a happy gathering. I'm Bill Headley." He had an expression on his face that suggested we should know who he was. I then realized he must be one of the County Commissioners that Mrs. Proctor had talked about at her campaign meeting. But what was he doing here—in District 1, at dusk, asking for

Reverend Lewis? He must have seen the glimmer of recognition in my face because he turned his smile on me.

I introduced myself and the others and explained that we were planning some silly entertainment for the Garden Fair that was coming up shortly.

"Why, yes, I've heard of it. I'll be sure to attend. It sounds like you're having great fun already."

I pointed him to the front of the Reverend's parsonage, and he walked across the back garden toward it. Freya waved her hand in front of her face as if she were overheated and her sister playfully slapped her hand.

"What cloud did he come down on?" Freya asked.

I imagined he drove in from Pittsfield like a normal human being. But what he was doing here was another question entirely.

Chapter 6

The next week was a flurry of activity, starting with a meeting of the Garden Fair group reporting back on Sunday afternoon. Mrs. Proctor was astonished at the extent to which we had fulfilled our assignments. Glenda and I were the joint entertainment committee organizers and, when it came time to report on what we had done, Glenda deferred to me, in part because she was a bit intimidated by Mrs. Proctor.

"We took your suggestion of entertainment a little further than what you might have intended," I began. "We've circulated a sign-up sheet for people who either play a musical instrument or sing and allotted ten minutes for each performance. You'd be surprised, but we have two and a half hours of entertainment available."

Mrs. Proctor and the other committee chairs were shocked. But positively.

"That's extraordinary!"

"We've got someone to put a small platform stage together for us and Mr. Ross, who everyone knows has a commanding voice, is in charge of announcing the performers. We don't have a microphone or anything, but I don't think we'll need one. We've got everything from the first-grade class reprising their Christmas carols from last December to a snake charmer."

The last mention drew gasps.

"Don't worry, it's not poisonous," I said with a smile.

"It's up to you how the performances are balanced with the judging of the categories and the announcements of the winners, but I think people who come will stay for several hours."

"Do you think we need to provide more food for sale, then?" Mrs. Rockmore asked.

"I should think so. It could raise quite a bit of money," Mrs. Proctor replied.

"The flyers for the Fair have been distributed to all the merchants here in town and also in Adams, and they have agreed to post them in their windows. I think that could attract a lot of people. Oh, and the Mountain Aire Hotel said they would transport guests who might like to attend," I added.

Now that Mrs. Proctor was suitably impressed by what we had accomplished, Glenda wanted a bit of the spotlight.

"We've got a pony ride set up and an enclosure for a petting zoo."

"A zoo?" Miss Olsen asked.

"A rabbit, a goat and some puppies. The Loughtons are hoping someone will want to take home a puppy."

"That's charming."

"And you created a baby zoo, didn't you?" I asked her with a smile.

"Yes, another enclosure in the soft grass in the shade for mothers and babies."

"Let's make sure they are labeled so nobody takes home the wrong baby," said Miss Olsen in all seriousness.

"I wouldn't want to mistake one of the puppies for Douglas," Glenda said. "Although a small dog must eat less than a hungry little boy."

Everyone laughed politely and it saved Miss Olsen's gaffe.

The meeting went on with reports from every committee and it sounded like it was turning out to be quite an event. The raffle items were cleverly services as well as actual things: Jassie's offered a wash and set, the Misses Smith a free alteration (although every woman knew how to sew and alter her clothes), two hours of babysitting from Mona Strathern—and I wondered if she had agreed to it or been strong-armed by her mother. The objects for the raffle were a strange combination of things nobody needed, like a milk glass bud vase, a tablecloth, a Foley food mill, costume jewelry, crocheted antimacassars, clothing and a hideous lamp that made it seem more of a rummage sale than a raffle. Of course, there were several volumes of Stuart Manley's books included.

"He'll be bringing up some of the young boys' books when he comes, too," Glenda added. I had suggested that he add things like a yo-yo, a ball, or other play items which might interest that audience to sweeten the pot as I was concerned that, in light of all the other things to do at the Garden Fair, entering a raffle for a book might not appeal to the youngsters, although I hoped I was wrong.

IT WAS a busy week for me as I fielded questions on the telephone and in person about some details of the Garden Fair while I was supposed to be working. John was patient about the distractions, telling me that it meant that people considered me one of the community. It only took me a year to achieve that distinction, despite hearing about the most personal health issues of everyone in town.

As the weather continued to warm up, we saw more people with hay fever for which there wasn't much remedy except a change in season, and that was some months away. Poison ivy reared its head as children played outside and the woods were full of it. One patient came in with a persistent rash on the outside of both of her calves and, after exhausting all explanations, it occurred to her that her dog often ran off to the woods and then came back home and brushed against her, releasing some of the irritating oils on her legs. The source of the rash. The only preventative was to remember to wash her skin as soon as he did this, bathe the dog frequently or wear pants. She chose the latter until fall came and the plants died back.

Sprains and strains were a frequent complaint and, with summer in full swing, farmers came in usually only when the pain got to an extreme level and then expected to be prescribed a liniment to solve the issue rather than giving the sore limb or joint a rest. Farming was hard in this rocky region with a short growing season, and they hated the notion of taking even a day off work.

One morning in Adams, John made an appointment with Mr. King at the bank to follow up on his loan request. He was full of enthusiasm and smiled at me with fingers crossed before he left. Of course, he would get the loan—the towns and surrounding area needed to support the growing practice of a young, energetic doctor since Doctor Mitchell had retired. And what better way to ensure that he would stay than to encourage him to put down solid roots in Adams by buying the building where the practice was located?

He returned in a foul mood, slapping the application papers down on my reception desk.

"Can you believe it? He didn't have the decency to talk to me! He sent his assistant out, some young flunky, to say that Mr. King had another meeting and wouldn't be able to accommodate me. I thought that meant I should reschedule, but the young pup turned red in the face and said that my application had been tabled."

"Tabled—what does that mean?" I asked for clarification.

"I thought he meant postponed and said that. He said, 'No, denied. If it were up to me....' Just like that." He snapped his fingers for emphasis. "And I said, 'Maybe someday it *will* be up to you.'"

Neither of us could know at that point how prescient John's comment was. Because before the week was out Mr. King was dead.

Chapter 7

When I got back to Miss Manley's, I couldn't help but share the news that John was refused a loan. I shook my head. "I can't understand the logic."

"It doesn't seem to make much sense. But where there's a will, there's a way, as my father used to say. He is well-liked in the community and will expand the practice with or without Mr. King."

"That's the spirit," I said, not feeling very confident at that moment.

"Remember, you said he has the contract at the Mountain Aire Hotel and the high school still wants him to do their sports physicals."

"Practically rolling in dough," I said.

The phone rang. It was Mrs. Proctor, who was able to track me down wherever I went to ask for some detail about the Fair that Saturday. Tensions were mounting as everyone was trying to stay on task for what turned out to be a more complex organizational enterprise than anticipated. I had to confess to myself that I had been part of the problem, suggesting the expansion of the entertainment component. Not only did we have more folks now who wanted to participate, but we also had people requesting time changes and wanting to swap places with those who didn't want to give up their slot. Oh, show business!

My more immediate concern was that my parents would be arriving on Friday to stay with Miss Manley, and I felt obligated to make sure they were attended to, as well, while keeping up my obligations with the Garden Fair. My mother told me that my father had twisted his knee somehow; the resultant injury and not being able to play golf put him in a grumpy mood. That, and having to use a cane, which she said he thought made him look ancient, almost had them cancel the trip. I did consider that he would be doing the driving up to West Adams and walking up and down the stairs and around the Fair. I hoped they could enjoy themselves as my father was rarely in a disagreeable mood.

The next morning in Adams was busy with patients and the telephone ringing with questions and requests to me that had nothing to do with medicine.

After the fourth call and John's scowling a bit at the noise and interruption, I was blunt.

"This will all be over this afternoon. Everyone knows to call me at Miss Manley's number until the last possible minute on Saturday with some imagined catastrophe of costuming or scheduling. If a performer does not show up, we'll just have silence."

"You must be joking! With all the people you expect—the babies, the children, the petting zoo, the violently competitive gardeners—it will be raucous chaos for hours."

"Maybe I should tell my parents not to come and I'll take the bus back home for the weekend," I suggested sweetly.

"Don't you dare! Mrs. Proctor will have your head on a platter if you even suggest it as a joke. It was a joke, wasn't it?"

"Of course. I wouldn't leave you and the snake hanging on stage alone."

"Snake?" Mr. Grimsby, the newest patient, looked around the reception room floor.

"Just teasing. No snakes here. I think," I said.

Nonetheless, he looked into the corners as he made his way to the exam room.

I was released from work as soon as we got back from Adams. The incessant phone calls and interruptions were driving us crazy, and John vowed he would not answer the phone at all.

"Let them figure out you're at home."

"Thanks. I want to make sure the room is ready for my parents." I walked home, zipped into our kitchen and saw Annie taking some pies from the oven.

"You didn't have to do that," I said.

She gave me the look that said, of course, she did and placed them on a cooling rack on the enamel-topped table.

I loved her cooking, but I also wanted the opportunity to take my parents to dinner that weekend at one of the area restaurants or perhaps the Mountain Aire. Miss Manley had already given Annie Saturday and Sunday off, so there would be no offense taken by her in doing so.

The phone rang and Annie said, "It has to be for you."

Glenda was in a tizzy because the man who was providing the portable wire fencing had dropped off a large roll in her driveway, blocking the garage where her car was parked.

"And he expects *me* to haul it to the Garden Fair site and set it up?"

"Calm down, I don't think so. He's from the nursery in Adams and he'll be back tomorrow to put it in place." I seemed to be saying the phrase, 'Calm down,' quite a bit lately.

"Well, then…."

"You won't need the car anyway since Stuart is driving his up later today."

"True. What are you all doing for dinner tonight?"

"My parents should be here soon, and Annie is making a pork roast that smells amazing and a couple of pies."

"Oh." She sounded forlorn and whispered, "Mrs. Nelson is making something very practical and awful. Something with cabbage that smells up the whole house. I don't think Stuart will be well pleased."

I wasn't in a position to invite her and her husband, much less the entire crew, over to Miss Manley's. They'd have to make do with what was provided. It made me wonder if Glenda was trying to cut corners by not providing enough in the household budget for the sort of food she would like to eat. I didn't know if she cooked much at all in the City, but I remembered that her interest in culinary matters was meager when she lived next door by herself the summer before.

"I've got to go," I said, cutting the conversation short. "We've agreed to get to the site early tomorrow, remember?"

"Ugh. Yes. See you then. Hello to Mother and Daddy," she said.

I checked the guest room next to mine and found that Annie had done her usual thorough job of preparing it. Then I changed out of my uniform and took a bath and allowed myself some moments of peace although I could hear the telephone ring a few times.

Sometime later, back downstairs, I looked for Miss Manley, who was in the sitting room with the French windows open to the late afternoon air.

"Aren't you going to cut the flowers and vegetables for the Fair tomorrow?" I asked.

She looked at me askance. "No, my dear. They need to be cut when the dew is still on them in the morning, just before we leave. I've got a small wagon in the garage and can bring them over close to opening time. Mrs. Rockmore thinks that her roses will be the show winner because she has a gardener and pumps the plants up with all kinds of additives. But mine have the perfect ratio of sun and shade. And of course, I get on my hands and knees and make sure the pests are not around them. I have heard that Mrs. Rockmore's gardener *sprays* her plants."

From her tone of voice, that was not the preferred method of dealing with whatever wanted to attack roses.

"DDT," she said, her mouth pursed in disapproval.

"Have you peeked over her garden wall to check out the competition?" I asked.

Miss Manley straightened her back and looked at me. I was sure she would deny it, but then she smiled. "Of course! I think I'll do quite well. My yellow beauty has such a depth of color, her pink ones can't hold a candle to it."

I put my head back to look through the hall and the dining room windows to see my parents' car pull up in the driveway.

"They're here."

I trotted out the back door and met them getting slowly out of the car as if they hadn't stopped the entire way up from Pelham. My mother sighed.

"What a long trip. But how scenic and what a lovely town." She kissed me and I could smell the lavender-scented soap that she used. She was considerably shorter than I and stouter but as good-humored as I was.

"Is that new?" I asked of the wide-brimmed, woven straw hat on her head.

"Yes, to keep the sun off, of course."

I turned to see what was taking my father so long and saw that he was struggling to get out of the car while wielding a cane with a knobby, carved handle. Finally upright, he hobbled over to me, all smiles.

"This darned knee," he said as he kissed me.

"I told you not to try all the new dances at once," I said.

"I think I'm supposed to say it is the bee's knees or something."

"Daddy, that's very old-fashioned. I'll make sure to introduce you to Reverend Lewis's nephew who lives next door. He knows all the current slang."

"Hmm," he grunted as he went to open the trunk.

"Dad, I'll get the bags. First, let's go inside and say hello to Miss Manley." I led them to the front of the house and through the proper entrance rather than the more familiar kitchen back door or French windows that I habitually used. My father was trying to keep up a brave face, but he was clearly in pain.

"How did you manage to do that?" I asked.

"Just turned suddenly and wrenched it out of place."

"Have you seen a doctor about it?"

He gave me a glance out of the corner of his eye indicating that he had not done so.

"If you'd like John to look at it, I'm sure he wouldn't mind." I got no response, but my mother just pursed her lips and shook her head. He was stoic but also stubborn.

It was a delightful reunion for my parents and Miss Manley, who had last seen each other at the Valentine Ball in Boston. Even though she was older, there were many commonalities of interest, and the conversation took off right away. I excused myself to get their suitcases from the car and place them in the hallway, then brought in the tea-things from the kitchen. I felt Annie had her hands full with the feast to come.

"Where is Doctor Taylor?" my mother asked.

"Still working. He'll be here for dinner. He let me off early because you were coming."

"And to answer all the calls about the Garden Fair," Miss Manley added with a smile.

"That's what all that business was as we were coming into town. Is it a carnival or something?" my father asked.

I had to laugh. "Yes, it seems like a circus, all right! It may be small potatoes, but it is a major event around here. I'm afraid I took my volunteer assignment too seriously and it may have got out of hand."

"What do you mean?" my mother sounded alarmed.

"Only that we opened the door on every amateur talent in the county. We had two spoon players and unfortunately could only accept the first applicant."

That got a giggle from my mother. "I didn't know people did that anymore."

"The original intent of the Garden Fair was to show off the flowers, plants and vegetables like a county fair on a small scale. But now it seems to have grown into something larger."

"Miss Manley, I didn't tell you, but it seems the County Commissioners—all three—have let us know they plan to attend. To 'glad hand' or whatever the expression is."

"Oh, dear. That changes the tenor of the event. Well, just be sure to sell them the maximum number of raffle tickets." There was a glint in her eye.

"There will be food available for sale this year and, since the Fair will last longer, it seems that there will be more income for the church funds. My father told me that back in the day when there were taverns, the owners would provide food when the patrons bought a beer. The saltier the food, the more likely they would be to buy another."

"Miss Manley, that's brilliant! I wish we had known that and, instead of ladylike sandwiches, we should have provided pretzels and salted peanuts."

"But you're not selling alcohol, I hope," my mother commented.

"Of course not. But thirst can be quenched with lemonade, too," I said.

There was a knock on the jamb of the French windows and John came in to greet my parents. They seemed to be fond of him, and I loved how he interacted so naturally with them.

"Good evening, all," he said. "The last patient left some time ago, so I locked up a tad early. People know how to find me if there is an emergency."

Which there seldom was.

"Mr. Burnside—a cane? I hope you haven't suffered an injury?"

"I wish I could claim that I had been attempting some daring athletic feat. Alas, I just twisted my knee, and it still hurts like the devil."

"I would be happy to look at it for you if you don't think that is too forward of me."

"Not at all," my father said. My mother and I exchanged knowing glances.

"How about tomorrow after the Grand Event of West Adams?"

"That suits me fine."

We were able to enjoy tea and conversation without the telephone ringing before John went back home to change for dinner and my parents got settled in their room and freshened up.

I was just going upstairs myself when the front doorbell rang, an unusual sound since most neighbors came around the back. I turned around and opened the door to Mrs. Proctor, who had a paper bag with rolls of raffle tickets and a zippered one with change for those who purchased them.

She put them in my arms and said rather dramatically, "You'll never guess what I just found out." Before getting a chance to respond, she went on with fury in her eyes. "I went into Pittsfield to buy these and bumped into my friend Margaret who works in the county offices. We are Daughters of the Nile, me through my husband and she through her father. Anyway, as we chatted, I told her that I was running for County Commissioner and that I thought one of the important issues was repairing the bridge near the Rosses' property. Then she said to me how interesting it was because Mr. King had just purchased land adjacent to that bridge!"

She was incensed but I didn't know why. The last time she had spoken about the bridge she said that Mr. King had no interest in its repair. So why had he bought property there? I suppose I looked blankly at her comments because she put on a sly smile.

"Young lady, you'll see what happens next." She nodded, turned on her heel and left.

As I ascended the stairs, Miss Manley was coming down.

"Who was that?"

"Mrs. Proctor. She had some things to give me including a cryptic message." In answer to her quizzical look, I shook my head in ignorance. "I'll just put these in my room and be down in a minute."

The weather was so mild that we decided to sit out in the back garden before dinner. My father had managed to bring a bottle of wine, which wasn't so hard to obtain if you claimed it was for religious purposes. Why anyone would use an aged red wine for communion or a Seder was beyond me, but it was one way around Prohibition and it was infinitely better than the medicinal elderberry wine Miss Manley brewed.

John appeared with a plate of hors d'oeuvres that Elsie, Nina's cook, had prepared as she knew that Annie would have her hands full with the lot of us and dinner as well.

"She was very particular that we partake of what she called these canopies," he said seriously. "Stuffed celery, anchovy crackers and candied walnuts."

We made the appropriate appreciative noises and helped ourselves to the unexpected bounty.

"Ready for tomorrow?" John asked me.

"I'll be ready for tomorrow night, I can tell you. By the way, I thought it would be a good idea for us to go out to dinner. Mother and Daddy haven't been to the Mountain Aire and we really should show them our patronage."

"Excellent idea," John said. "My treat."

I knew that was polite of him as the local host, but I worried about the expense. I wish I hadn't been so attuned to financial matters, but that was my nature.

"What have you got planned for us tomorrow?" my mother asked.

"The excitement of a county fair on a smaller scale," John answered. "No livestock showing—that is saved for the Berkshire County Fair in the fall. This is an entirely local affair, with stiff competition among the neighbors for who grew the best plants and vegetables."

"You can try to make fun of us, Doctor Taylor, but we take our horticultural endeavors seriously. After all, we have a long winter and a short summer in which to produce those living things that consume much of our attention and energy," Miss Manley said.

She might have been talking about a litter of pigs, but she was referring, of course, to her roses, which were her pride and joy.

"I'm afraid I have been a rather helpless gardener," my mother said. "We have shrubs around the house and at the perimeter of the property and then a lawn. I've often thought about planting daisies or something, but I'm ignorant of the process."

"I would be happy to give you some seeds and some tips on how best to cultivate them. It's not difficult, just a matter of knowing how to do it."

"That would be lovely," my mother said, looking at my father in a way that told me she hadn't expected that response and then felt the obligation of trying her hand at it. What was the worst that could happen? The seeds would sprout or they wouldn't. She could attribute success or failure to the different climate in Westchester County.

"The most important thing tomorrow is to see Glenda and the baby. She will be holding court in something they are calling a baby pen, a fenced grassy area under the trees where mothers and small children can be contained. He's a hearty little boy and she is enormously proud to show him off."

We talked about Glenda's temporary relocation for the summer, Stuart's thriving publishing business and the new endeavor of books for boys based in part on those he had already written for adults.

"You'll get to meet the Crompton sisters, too, who are part of Stuart's burgeoning literary empire," John said. "They talk a mile a minute, which is fun to listen to, and type at the same speed and extreme velocity, which is not as pleasant."

"I don't think I told you, but the Crompton sisters have a funny fortune-telling routine that they will be doing," I said to Miss Manley.

"For the price of a raffle ticket, I hope," Miss Manley said.

"But of course. They have scarves on their head, jangly jewelry, exotic makeup, absurd accents and, of course, no expertise in telling the future. But I'm sure it will be an amusing exercise for people to have their palms read."

"Oh, my. I remember doing something like that many years ago at a carnival. Of course, I was a young girl, and all the predictions were so intriguing. A handsome young man, a change of scene, a trip, et cetera. I'm sure the woman said the same thing to everyone who saw her, but that didn't occur to me. And wouldn't you know it, I exited her tent and there before me was a very handsome man! It turned out to be one of the carnival barkers, a most unsuitable person for me to be associated with, but still, she had predicted my future! And then, still in the thrall of her powerful voice and manner, there was a change in my life. We got a new neighbor." She laughed. "That was to be expected since the house next to ours had been empty for some time. And the trip! That was to the faraway location of Vermont—it makes me laugh to imagine that I was so naïve to believe all that nonsense. But it was harmless in retrospect."

"I think they have the good sense to tell the fortunes with the age of the customers in mind. And if they tell me I am going on a long trip, I'll want to know where first."

"I'll settle for the prediction of a sudden financial fortune coming my way," John said.

I couldn't agree more.

Chapter 8

In retrospect, I thought it curious that no men were involved in the planning and execution of the Garden Fair—except for hauling tables and chairs and assembling the enclosures for the children and the petting zoo, when they were at the beck and call of the women who organized the event. Had this been the town tradition for as long as anyone could remember? Or because everyone assumed women were better at detail or minutiae? Whatever the reason, the men were lucky not to be involved in small squabbles about the placement of bunting around a table or whether the flowers exhibited should be in a straight line or staggered—the issue being one of fairness versus artistic design.

Even stranger was that the entire process of designing and executing what was a complex event for a small town was not more admired or respected. Mrs. Proctor had ably shown her leadership skills, organizational ability, financial acumen and cajoling prowess in pulling this all together seamlessly. Yet when it came to running for County Commissioner, the assumption was that the male candidates were the preferred variety. I hadn't had any interactions with Mr. King and, although I knew he was president of the bank in Adams, I knew nothing about his other capabilities. The same went for my assessment of the other two Commissioners' abilities. And I had been oblivious to what occurred at their meetings or how they spent the taxpayers' money. Why shouldn't she be considered as competent as they?

As a result, after all the effort she put into the Garden Fair, she found it irksome that the three Commissioners appeared early to the grounds and asked if they could be of any help. Of course, they could, but it was a bit late for that and, of all the people in attendance, they were the only ones in dress clothes. Although they worked regularly together, it was clear that there was no great camaraderie among them; Mr. King, the smaller man, seemed to try to exert his dominance over the other two by speaking first and more loudly. Headley and Campbell looked peeved but did not interrupt. He indicated that they had the intention of electioneering during the event, not asking for permission but stating their intention. I had come to know her well enough to recognize the barely disguised irritation in her demeanor as she faced the trio, who probably thought it best to approach her as one. She was polite but firm that the interactions be limited, even though there would be no way for her to enforce it. She turned on her heel and I thought I could see a plan hatching in her brain.

Things came together quickly with the floral competitors having placed their prize flowers in various sized containers on the tables, some decorated with ribbons and bows. Miss Manley had brought three of her butter yellow roses in a tall clear vase that showed off their beauty and perfect form. No frou-frous for her to enhance the judges. Then I remembered that I was one of the judges. Although the identity of each contestant was on a card face down behind their exhibit, would everyone assume I would favor Miss Manley's roses, having seen them growing and lovingly tended each day? I decided I would defer to the other judges and then concur with them to prevent any hint of favoritism.

Several other long tables supported the vegetable and house plant entries, both harder to identify by the owner. It looked as if some had a touch of oil applied to the foliage to give them a sheen in the early morning sun.

"Mrs. Proctor, when do we do the judging?"

"I would say that you, Mr. Bridges and Reverend Lewis should start the process about ten o'clock, while everything is fresh, and the announcement can be made shortly before eleven. We hope that people will begin eating shortly thereafter."

There was a sudden influx of people, most of whom I didn't recognize, so I assumed they had come from Adams and outlying areas. The idea of posting flyers had been a good one. After a short time, a smaller group appeared from the Mountain Aire, as I recognized Bernard and Catherine, the two assistants to Cash Ridley, who was ensconced there for the summer. I waved to them and wanted to have a chat, but as the person in charge of the entertainment that started at eleven, I had to make sure that Miss Ballantine was stationed to check in each performer in turn.

After being reassured that the performances were in order, my eye was caught by a small tent erected a short way from the main activity that was not in the original plan, and I went to see what it was. Tacked on the outside was a handwritten sign in scrawling letters that said:

Explore your past, Recognize the present, See the future

Madame Celestia, Fortuneteller Extraordinaire

Inside was a small table, a glass orb and two chairs with one of the Crompton sisters seated behind. Her face was so disguised that I couldn't tell which one it was at first.

"Freya?" I asked.

"Vat do you think of my outfit?" she asked, shaking her hands that made the metal canning jar lids on her wrists jingle.

"That's very good," I said, commenting on the ingenuity of her costume, the curtain ring earring dangling from a string around her ear, the multitude of scarves and beads that adorned her head and neck and Glenda's mother's ruffled blouse. "Where did you get the dark makeup?"

"Glenda had it in the attic leftover from a high school production of the Pirates of Penzance."

"I gather she was one of the pirates?"

"The king."

"The things I don't know about Glenda," I muttered. Still, the orangey-brown tint was a good disguise, not that many people in the town had met the sisters.

"How many raffle tickets for a fortune?" she asked.

"Let's say two. They are pretty cheap, to begin with. And we want people to value your abilities to predict the future."

"Vould you like to be my first?"

"I'll be back later, Freya. Mrs. Proctor has some other chores for me."

"That's why we're hiding out here," Minerva, who had been lying out of sight on the ground behind her sister, said. She too was in full makeup and garish clothes. Very smart of them: they could take turns, and no one would be the wiser.

I checked my watch and realized I should be gathering the other two judges and deciding how we would do this process. In the meantime, people were milling about the tables, exclaiming over a beautiful, deep purple eggplant, an early arrival for this time in the summer. I heard someone whisper to her friend, "Hothouse, I'll bet."

Interesting. Were hothouse plants and flowers considered borderline cheating? What about those protected from pests and disease with powders or sprays? Should there be a table for the naturally grown versus those that might have had the help of a glass shelter or soil amendments? That might be a discussion for next year's event. I rounded up Mr. Bridges and the Reverend and pulled them aside, giving them the small notepads and pencils that Mrs. Proctor had provided. They looked down at them curiously.

"We should take notes, after all. What are the criteria for judging?" I asked.

The men looked at each other.

"I'd like to say the best one wins," Mr. Bridges offered.

"Perhaps we need to take into consideration color, shape and fragrance, if there should be one," the Reverend added.

"Let's add presentation and I don't know what you'd call it, but whether it is the best example of the plant. You know, like animals are judged. A geranium should look like the best geranium," I said.

"Do we tally points?"

My shoulders slumped. This was getting complicated. "Why don't we each look them over, take notes and then compare. I bet we'll have some consensus." I hoped this would not be a long morning.

As we proceeded down the line of cut flowers it occurred to me that I didn't know the names of many of them, therefore how could I judge which was the best whatever it was? I hoped that when the cards were turned over it would be clear what we had ascertained was the best of its kind.

West Adams people loved to garden, that was obvious, and were proud of their accomplishments. While I always admired flowering plants, I realized I was woefully ignorant of what many were called. There were daisies, black-eyed Susans and marigolds, and I recognized peonies from their globe-shaped flowers and sweet smell. That ended my ability to identify floral species and I vowed that, if I did this task next year, I would be better prepared. There were lots of pink and red roses, some garnished with babies' breath to bring out the color. The hydrangeas were plentiful—some pink, some blue and some greenish white, which I didn't think was very attractive. As we moved along, I thought we might be able to award the best large, cut flower and best smaller variety allowing for more winners. The non-blooming plants were a separate category, easily divided into houseplant and outdoor plants. And the vegetables could stay in their division.

With that in mind, we retired to the shade of a maple and began our deliberations. I let the men lead with their comments in the small flower class and was happy to know that the yellow roses were the clear winner. I concurred, and if challenged could admit that I had followed their lead. The other winners involved a bit more debate, as there were more of them in contention, but after a few minutes, we had our roster and just in time as Mrs. Proctor was striding our way.

"We're ready," I said, taking a detour to the tables to pick up the cards that identified the winners, and she led us toward the small stage that had been set up.

"So, you're the tall drink of water that I've heard so much about," said a smarmy voice as I walked through the crowd.

"Excuse me?" I said, looking around to see who had spoken to me.

"Mr. King," the man said, holding out his hand to me.

I was so flustered as I looked down at the lewd smile on the broad face of the short man that I didn't respond or shake his hand. If I were a tall drink of water, he was a short tumbler. He couldn't possibly be the banker!

My parents stood nearby and were obviously as shocked by his comment as I was. We judges made our way to the small stage where Mrs. Proctor was already standing and calling for attention from the crowd.

"Ladies and gentlemen! May I have your attention?" It was more a command than a question, and the noise diminished except for a lonesome bleat from a billy goat and the vocalizations of the infant humans as they sat with their mothers in the shade.

"Welcome to the Garden Fair." Applause followed. "You can see we have a larger event than in years past and it is due to the tireless work of the women of West Adams. Please give them a warm round of applause." The crowd obeyed.

"The first event of the day is awarding the prizes for the spectacular floral and vegetable displays." More applause. "The judges will now announce the winners."

At that moment, we realized that we didn't have the ribbon rosettes to hand out. Miss Olsen bustled up to the stage with them in her hands and gave them to Mrs. Proctor. We had decided that each judge would announce the winner in one category, making sure that I was not the one to call out Miss Manley's name. With each announcement read from the cards we had plucked from the tables, there was subdued clapping and I later learned that the same people usually won in each category every year, no matter who was judging. Our job done, we left the stage and Mrs. Proctor invited everyone to buy raffle tickets to pay for the food, the games and the assortment of items for sale. She then gestured to Mr. Ross, who had been enlisted to announce the entertainers. While he struggled with his glasses to read off the list, Mr. King jumped onto the stage, smiling broadly and welcoming the crowd as though he had invited them.

"Welcome everyone, thank you for coming! I'm Tony King, your County Commissioner. And I'd like to bring up my fellow commissioners—come on up—Bill Headley, District 2 and Jesse Campbell, District 3." There was polite applause.

I turned to look at Mrs. Proctor, whose face was like thunderclouds as this little man presumed to coopt the loyalty of the people she had worked so hard to get to attend the most important event in West Adams. If he noticed her displeasure, he didn't show it and continued to talk about what they had done for Berkshire County and West Adams in particular. I heard Mrs. Proctor sniff in derision at that declaration. Then he went into a long description of projects in other parts of the county that were of direct benefit to us all. Just as he was winding down, Mr. Headley, the handsome one, took up the baton and continued to outline policies that had been passed that were intended to bring more commerce and tourism to the area. He motioned to Mr. Campbell who carried on in the same vein. Mr. Ross was standing awkwardly on the stage, wondering when they would stop talking, and shrugged, which got a huge laugh from the crowd. Taking that as a sign to stop campaigning, the three Commissioners congratulated the winners and waving, left the stage.

Mr. Ross cleared his throat and announced the first act, a brother and sister flute and violin duet. The Commissioners passed through the crowd nodding and shaking hands, but Mrs. Proctor was having none of it. To the strains of **Für Elise** coming from the stage, she poked her index finger in Mr. King's chest.

"How dare you! Using this social occasion as a personal campaign event?"

Mr. King kept a smile on his face. "Thank you, Mrs. Porter, how nice to see you." He barreled on through the throng and I had to admire his brazen lack of conscience.

"Mrs. *Proctor*!" she said loudly to his back, but he was too busy glad-handing his way toward the food tent.

John caught my arm and commented on my surprised face.

"That odious little man!" I said.

"Which one?" he asked in all seriousness, but it made me laugh, and I let it go.

"Never mind. We've got about an hour until our performance comes up. Let me check on my parents and see that they have got a place to sit down."

They had found chairs near the baby zoo, as Glenda called it, under the trees that marked the end of the cultivated lawn where a ditch lay beyond. She was talking to them from one side of the fencing holding onto Douglas's hands while he tried deep knee bends and laughed. It was amazing the amount of energy babies expended—no wonder they needed so many naps.

"He's just precious," my mother said, looking from him to me. Anyone else would have thought she was seeking my agreement, but I knew that she was wondering when I would produce a grandchild.

My father rubbed his knee and asked me, "What was that man saying to you?"

"I believe he thought he was complimenting me on my height."

"It sounded downright disrespectful," my father said with a frown.

"Who?" John asked.

"Your Mr. King," I said.

My father shot him a look.

"Who said he is *my* Mr. King? He's the man who refused me a business loan, remember?"

"Maybe I should have gone in with you to ask for the loan," I said in jest.

"Agnes, what a horrible suggestion," my father said.

"Just joking, Dad. Really."

"Look at those popinjays," he said.

I pulled John aside and whispered, "He must be in a lot of pain. I have never seen him in such an unpleasant mood."

"I'd be happy to take a look at it later today. When all the fun and festivities are over, of course."

"I'm having fun. Sort of. You wouldn't think such a small affair would consume so many hours of planning and execution. And it's not even noon!"

We went to the refreshment tent, and I got sandwiches for my parents and Glenda while John bought some drinks. Once delivered, we returned to get portions for ourselves and were glad we beat the rest of the crowd as the supplies were dwindling by then.

After our brief meal, I left John with my parents while I visited the fortune-telling tent that finally had no line waiting outside.

"Oh, Madame Celestia?" I sang out and drew back the tent flap. To my surprise, one of the sisters was in an embrace with Mr. Headley.

"Excuse me," I said and stumbled out smack into Mrs. Rockmore.

"Was it fun?" she asked, giggling at the thought of having her fortune told.

"Unexpected, I would say." I nodded as she looked at me in puzzlement.

A clearing of the throat indicated that Mr. Headley had exited the tent, wiping his face with his handkerchief, trying to get the lipstick and orangey makeup off his face.

"Oh!" said Mrs. Rockmore.

I walked away shaking my head and decided I could do without knowing my future today.

The spoon players were surprisingly good, and before that day I did not know it was a musical art form of some sort. We were treated to an accordion concerto, some hymn singing by the church choir and the first-grade class with their reprisal of Christmas carols. I looked at my watch and got John so we could change for our performance.

I was more nervous about this silly skit than I had been at either of my two graduation ceremonies. It was ridiculous, but on with the show, I thought. I had changed into my nurse's uniform, John had put on his white coat and brought his stethoscope and I carried a large round basket with Moe the snake inside.

When it was our turn, John got on the stage and sat down while I brought the basket up and put it on the ground.

"What's that?" he asked.

"Your next patient," I answered.

"Rather small, isn't he?"

"I would say he was rather long, instead."

The audience giggled and kept their eyes on the basket.

"Can you get him out?"

"I think you had better do that," I said.

He stood up, slowly lifted the lid of the basket and slammed it down again with a yelp.

It got a great laugh from the crowd.

"It's a snake!" he shouted.

I think some of the audience wondered if there was a live snake in the basket. In the second row was the patient from the Adams' office when we were discussing snakes in the reception room, and he was nodding his head up and down in affirmation.

"Where are Susie and her flute?" he asked. He was referring to the girl who had played a duet with her brother at the beginning of the entertainment. He had set this bit up himself with her earlier.

"There she is. Perhaps if you could play something, he might come out."

She obliged and funnily tootled on her flute.

Nothing happened. John and Susie looked at one another and she gave it another try.

Still nothing.

"Thanks, Susie. It looks like I'll just have to go it alone."

"Be careful, Doctor Taylor!" I said, with fear in my voice.

He strode to the basket, lifted the lid, reached in and wrestled with both hands, emerging with the ridiculous stuffed snake with its googly eyes and red felt tongue hanging out.

There was surprise and relief from everyone, and they laughed when they saw how improbable a scene was about to take place.

John sat back down and looked at the snake's face which had turned to him with the help of the human hand inside.

"What's your name?"

"Moe." It was that falsetto voice that John used, and his lips moved as the snake talked which made it even funnier.

"Is that your only name?"

"No."

"How are you feeling?"

"So-so." He made the snake's face turn to the crowd, and they laughed again.

"Nurse, let's take his temperature."

I put a straw in the snake's mouth and took it out almost immediately.

"Oh my, it looks like he has a sore throat."

That was the end of my part of the performance, and I stepped off the stage while John continued a nonsensical conversation with the snake who would only respond in one-word answers that rhymed with 'no.' As John went on, the crowd could anticipate what word was going to be said, for instance, 'what do you like about winter' and some children shouted out, 'snow.'

As the performance time expired, John said, "I'm afraid I can't do anything more for you." He stood up and said, "It's time for you to …."

"Go!" the children shouted and John threw the snake into the audience, resulting in squealing and laughing. He bowed to the rowdy clapping and retrieved his snake before it was man-handled by the children.

"Phew, I was running out of words," he said.

"So?" I said.

"Very funny. We should book ourselves into the Mountain Aire as a local vaudeville troupe."

"We'd have to come up with a longer routine, as well as song and dance."

"I think we'd better stick with medicine."

"Yes, that's a much better plan."

Chapter 9

The Garden Fair was a big hit and well attended. And as John had predicted, it was raucous and chaotic. The petting zoo fence was knocked down by one of the goats, and there was a hilarious chase through the crowds with everyone reaching hands out to try to catch it. One of the Connelly boys grabbed it around the neck and wrestled it to the ground like a steer in a rodeo event and there was a loud cheer, followed by the sounds of at least one baby crying at the noise. The bean bag toss and other games got their fair share of participants. But the Loughtons' puppies were even more popular than the petting zoo and the bane of many parents. I can't remember how many times I heard the exchange where the child was saying, 'Please, please' and the parent's exasperated response inquiring who was going to feed it. Despite those protests, all six were in the happy arms of youngsters before one o'clock.

We only had a half hour more of the festivities and the entertainment was winding down, with some farmer on stage executing a series of strange whistles. I never got an explanation of what that was about, and I was too tired to care. I knew that, once everyone left, there would still be the task of packing and cleaning up, although I hoped some of the tasks could wait until the next day. I suggested this to Mrs. Proctor as a way of lightening her mood, but it wasn't to be.

"Of course not. We can't leave the tables and chairs, the tents and fencing up! We don't want it to look like a carnival was here and was run out of town. And it might rain."

I nodded but was not in agreement.

Mr. King came up too close beside me and, putting his hand on my waist, said, "Goodbye, ladies. I hope we'll see each other again." He smiled at me and Mrs. Proctor mockingly, and her resolve cracked.

"J'accuse!" she shouted at him, pointing her index finger.

Everything except the whistling from the stage came to a silent standstill. Mr. King gaped at her.

"J'accuse!" she said again, pointing at him, her finger shaking in fury.

Miss Olsen at my elbow whispered to me, "Who is Jack Hughes?"

"You don't belong in public office. I know for a fact that there have been some shenanigans from you and your fellow commissioners. A bunch of hooligans."

"What are you talking about?"

"Kickbacks is what I'm talking about."

He scoffed and turned away.

Out of the corner of my eye, I could see my father hobbling forward, with my mother trying to restrain him. I didn't know if he was trying to protect me and Mrs. Proctor, prevent an altercation or just observe more closely what was transpiring.

"And I know you bought the property next to the bridge that is falling. At a reduced price, from what I hear. You've been ignoring that bridge for years and now I bet the county will suddenly find the funds to do something about it."

Mr. King turned back and spat out, "You miserable hag. You need to learn the rules of decency and campaigning before hurling insults and accusations. It's called defamation."

He strode through the crowd confidently, his mouth set with the certainty that no one would believe her.

Mrs. Proctor practically fell into my arms, still shaking with anger. "I'll see he doesn't do any further damage to our town."

A man came up and said, "Now, dear." It must have been Mr. Proctor, although I couldn't place him just then. He took her arm and led her away while the rest of us stood dumbstruck by the scene.

The crowd noise gradually increased from silence to murmuring and then conversation as if everyone by prior agreement knew the Garden Fair was over for the year. Contestants picked up their displays, the animals were herded out, the only children remaining in the baby zoo were two toddlers who had missed their nap, what was left of the food was carried out to waiting cars and, in a matter of twenty minutes, the entire area was devoid of all but the women who had organized it.

Miss Olsen clutched the zippered money pouch to her chest and said, "Where's Mrs. Proctor?"

"I think Mrs. Proctor would appreciate it if you dropped that off at her house soon. Judging by the heft of it, it looks like the Fair did very well. She'll be pleased."

Miss Olsen smiled. "It was going so well until that horrible man…."

"Yes, as we know, some men can be horrible."

I walked toward the stage, picking up napkins and trash as I went. The women who had brought the lawn games had folded them up while several men loaded them into the bed of a farmer's truck. As we cleaned up, other women scanned the lawn and came away with a scarf and a potted plant that had been left behind on the display table. They all looked as exhausted as I felt, and it seemed everything we could do had been done.

John was waiting for me by the collapsed food tent, his arms crossed over his chest.

"Well done. And it certainly ended with a bang."

"That's putting it mildly. I know it's only mid-afternoon, but it feels like I've been up for days."

He tucked my arm in his and we began to walk back to the main street and our respective homes.

"Why don't you have a bit of a nap before we go to dinner? Our reservation at the Mountain Aire is for seven and by that time, you'll be entirely refreshed and ready to dish the dirt on all that happened."

I liked his suggestion, and the walk through town with the light breeze blew away some of the tension of the day. He dropped me off at the French doors at Miss Manley's and I removed my nurse's cap that I had worn for the skit as I walked in. My parents were in the sitting room with my landlady drinking lemonade, and all of them looked tired.

"Congratulations on your winning submission!" I said.

"I feel you had something to do with it," she said.

"I was all too aware that if I took the lead on judging that category, someone might call foul. I let the Reverend and Mr. Bridges have their say first before I uttered a word. And, of course, it was unanimous."

She beamed at that.

"Your roses were exquisite," my mother said. "And their presentation in its simplicity made them stand out even more."

Now Miss Manley was blushing.

"It's true," I said. "Now, after a long day, I will put my feet up, have a bit of a rest and we'll leave for the Mountain Aire about six-thirty.

Mother, Dad, feel free to do the same." My father stood up, holding onto the arm of the chair.

"Dad, where is your cane?"

"Do you know, I am so opposed to having to use one that I often leave it behind. We drove over to the Garden Fair even though it's not very far. I'm sure it's in the car. We'll get it later."

EVEN A SHORT NAP can be so restorative, and I woke with plenty of time to prepare for dinner. I looked in on my parents to make sure that they were up and about before returning to my room and changing into a mid-length dress suitable for the elegance of the Mountain Aire. It was a seasonal place filled with people in the spring, summer and fall and then almost empty in the winter. The Fosters kept it going in all seasons, however, as it was their livelihood and home, but winter visitors were few and skiers tended to stay farther north in Vermont, close to the slopes. I hadn't tried skiing yet and the thought of binding my feet onto wooden slats and careening down an icy hill was not appealing. John and his friend, Fred Browne, who lived in Boston, were skiers, and if they pressed me into it, I thought I might give it a try. But winter was months away and we had to hold close and enjoy every moment of this mild summer.

What I loved most about being so far north was that it was still light till almost nine o'clock in the summer. I wondered if the Mountain Aire had their terrace tables set up for dinner. It would be lovely to sit on the terrace and watch the fireflies twinkling in the night.

"Mother, you look lovely!" I said when she came into the sitting room.

"Don't act so surprised, dear. I've had some hints from a new neighbor and changed my wardrobe a bit. I'm trying not to look so dowdy."

"Don't be ridiculous. You could never look dowdy." With a full head of silvery hair swept up in her usual Gibson Girl hairdo, it softened her features and made her look youthful, not old. I heard my father stomping down the stairs and my mother made a face.

"He doesn't want to bring his cane," she whispered. "He says he can't find it."

"We won't be doing much walking. As long as he is not uncomfortable," I said.

"It has nothing to do with comfort and everything to do with appearance."

"Good evening, ladies," he said and lowered himself into a chair with some effort.

"I'll just see what's keeping Miss Manley," I said and went through the swinging door to the kitchen. "There you are."

She was putting the finishing touches on a delicate tray with the decanter of her elderberry wine, five aperitif glasses and a bowl of almonds. She wore a blue floral dress, one of several new items she had purchased in Boston in February, and it flattered her eyes and skin tone. I noticed she had also tried to replicate the more complicated hairstyle that my aunt's hairdresser had created for her for the Valentine Ball. It was less dramatic, but becoming, nonetheless.

"I'll get the tray for you," I said. She propped the door to the hall open with the doorstop and made her way to the sitting room. I took up the tray and turned to the sound of a tap on the back door and John's entry into the room.

"Good evening, beautiful," he said, kissing me on the cheek. "My, you even smell good enough to eat."

"Don't spoil your appetite before dinner," I teased him.

We went into the sitting room as the lowering sun cast fine beams of light across the carpeting, creating a scene that could have been a painting in a museum.

"What are you smiling about, dear?" my mother asked.

"It's wonderful to be among people I care for. I'm very happy today."

"And exhausted, I should think," Miss Manley added. She poured out portions of wine for us all. I confess I was beginning to get used to it, although I preferred gin.

"We're only missing Glenda, Stuart and little Douglas," my mother said.

"Don't worry. She's making Sunday dinner for us all tomorrow." In answer to Miss Manley's anxious look, I added, "Mrs. Nelson will be helping her." I hoped it wasn't going to be a cauldron of baked beans and tinned meat.

John stood up. "Here's to the grand prize winner in the floral category." He nodded at Miss Manley, who was justifiably proud. "And to the lovely Agnes Burnside, who devoted so many hours to the betterment of the community. And she's only been in it one year. Here, here."

"It may have looked like devotion, but there was a fair bit of strong-arming, as well."

"It doesn't matter. It was all for the good of West Adams."

I drank my tiny tumbler of wine and excused myself to get a shawl, as it would be cooler at the hotel. Then I thought, yes, I had been here a little more than one year and so much had happened. Now we were off to the Mountain Aire Hotel, where I expected we might see Cash Ridley, that bombastic financier who had almost purchased the place last year. Glenda said he was back for a month and, as he was one of Stuart's investors, she was probably right.

"Shall I drive?" my father asked.

"No, no," John insisted. "My car is comfortable enough for all five of us. And of course, I know the way." We stood up to leave.

"Let me just lock our car," my father said and the three of us laughed.

"Mr. Burnside, this is West Adams," Miss Manley said. "Nothing ever happens here."

Well, almost nothing.

The Mountain Aire shone like a beacon in the little valley where it sat, its tennis courts and swimming pool visible as we came off the ridge and down the drive.

"Oh, it's lovely," my mother said.

"And very upscale for the area. Most people who vacation here stay in cabins or motor courts but this, as you can see, is a step above."

"I hope it's not too expensive," she said quietly to my father.

I knew John was paying for us all, and, yes, it was costly, but he wanted to show that he could afford such a luxury from time to time, and my mother's reaction was characteristic of her caution about the wolf at the door.

We were able to eat on the terrace and heard the strains of the sedate band inside; it seemed the Mountain Aire was done with jazzy singers for the time being. Our meal was leisurely and delicious, with my father not too casually asking John about the practice and juggling the two locations. I listened as John explained his desire to expand the practice with possibly a new location or new equipment, never mentioning the issue of the loan. It wasn't untruthful but not an entirely honest explanation of the state of things. Although he was under no obligation to put all his cards on the table, John very deftly maneuvered the dialogue to my father's work, and it seemed he had avoided a slightly uncomfortable conversation. I noticed Miss Manley looking down at her dessert plate rather than at the speakers.

It was a lovely evening after a hectic day, and on the ride back home all I could think was there was nothing to get up early for the next day. Except for church at ten o'clock, a reasonable time for a service, where I could introduce my parents to some of our neighbors. John was right, I was beginning to feel like this was my environment, my town, my people.

We pulled into the driveway to see Officer Reed's car parked behind my parents' vehicle. What could he want from Miss Manley or us at this time of night?

Very politely, he removed his hat and introduced himself and let us know that he was here for Doctor Taylor.

"I noticed he was not at home nor were you, so I asked at Mrs. Glenda Manley's house next door, and she mentioned you were out for the evening."

Why was he being so purposefully vague?

He pulled John aside and said in a whisper that, of course, we could all hear, "Doctor Taylor, I'm afraid there's been a death I need you to help me with."

Chapter 10

My immediate reaction was to ask who it was and how it happened, since by his presence and his wording it wasn't either an expected passing or the result of some illness. I knew better than to say anything at that point and John would tell me everything in the morning, but what an awful end to an otherwise wonderful evening. We solemnly trooped into the house while John and Officer Reed left in his car.

"Would anyone like coffee or tea?" Miss Manley asked.

We all demurred, having had a full meal, dessert and coffee at the Mountain Aire, but we proceeded into the sitting room and sat to contemplate what might have occurred.

"Do the police usually ask Doctor Taylor to be present after any death in the area?" my mother asked.

"If it were one of his patients, the family usually calls his office, but he wasn't there to answer. That could be one reason. If someone dies unexpectedly, he is called to fill out a death certificate."

"And there could be other reasons, too," my father said.

"Yes, as a lawyer would know, the officials tend to want a physician at the scene of a suspicious death to determine if there were natural causes."

My mother looked perplexed. "Which do you think it is?"

"I have no idea. I expect we'll know in the morning."

"Oh, dear."

"I don't want to make light of what might be a sad or upsetting issue, but since we don't know any more than that, why don't we discuss something more pleasant?" my father asked.

That was a familiar phrase in our home when something difficult had happened or one of us was in a mood and challenged the others: 'Why don't we discuss something more pleasant.'

"Shall we have a review of the food?" I asked.

My mother jumped right in. "The lamb was so tender and succulent and the sauce—I can't quite make out what the ingredients were, but it added depth and flavor."

"They do have an excellent chef this year, I am told," Miss Manley said, picking up her knitting basket and reaching in for her latest project, some small, off-white thing.

"That must be a difficult business, running a hotel and dining room," my father said.

"There is also a large banquet room where they have a band and dancing on the weekends. That was the music we could overhear outside. But you're right, the Fosters work hard to maintain the property, entertain the guests, pamper them, feed them and whatever else they do to make them happy."

"The hotel has been there for a long time, but the Fosters have upgraded it significantly in the past few years," Miss Manley added. "It must have been a challenge doing it while the Crash was taking its toll on everyone's wallet. But as it turned out, many of the wealthy retained their wealth, if not their way of living, and business has hardly suffered. It was there just last year that my nephew, Stuart, with whom we'll have dinner tomorrow, met Cash Ridley, a very wealthy businessman who has now become an investor in his company."

"Which is that?" my father asked.

"Hastings and Manley. Publishers. My nephew is a prolific author of adventure fiction books and has expanded into publishing for younger people."

"What an excellent idea," my mother said. "Would Eddie know any of the titles?" she asked me.

"I don't think so. They're mostly for youngsters, not young men."

The conversation rattled around for a bit about what my younger brother Eddie was doing and the current occupations of my cousins Amanda and Louisa, whom we had just visited in February for a debutante ball in Boston, and then suddenly everyone ran out of steam.

"I'm sorry to excuse myself, Miss Manley, but I am so tired from the long day," my mother said. She and my father said their goodnights and went up to bed. I wanted to stay and let Miss Manley know of all the shenanigans she may have missed at the Garden Fair.

"I may not have been very visible to everyone, but I certainly heard a great deal, especially Mrs. Proctor's accusation toward Mr. King. She's a forceful woman but usually self-contained. I can't imagine what led to that outburst."

Then I told her the tidbit of information that Mrs. Proctor shared with me the night before and her eyes widened.

"That's very interesting. I wonder if the information is correct. Folks often like to point their fingers at people in positions of power. And he has not conducted himself as well as he should have since being elected."

"Speaking of which," I said, lowering my voice. "I went to get my fortune read and came upon one of the Crompton sisters in an embrace with Mr. Headley."

At this, Miss Manley put down her knitting needles. "I know the sisters have been a valuable addition to Stuart's business and they can be a lively twosome. But there has already been gossip about what goes on in the Reverend's shed besides typing." She picked up the needles again. I was dying to ask her to elaborate but knew by her silence that she was not going to tell me more at that point. I smiled to myself. She would let this slip out in time. I just had to wait.

THE NEXT MORNING, I was awakened by the doorbell ringing. This was odd on two accounts: people who knew us well didn't come to the front door or ring the doorbell, they came around to the back to the kitchen door where Annie would admit them. Then I remembered that Miss Manley had given Annie the day off. Having the bedroom closest to the top of the stairs, I hastily slid my feet into slippers, put my arms through the sleeves of the robe and was tying it closed when the bell rang again.

I opened the door to Officer Reed, who looked uncomfortable and had a hard time meeting my eyes.

"Goodness, has something happened to John?" The last time I saw him, he had taken John away to certify a death and I imagined something awful had occurred to him.

"No, Miss, not at all. And I apologize for the early hour."

"What time is it?"

"It's seven-thirty. I just wanted to make sure that all of you in the household would be here a little later this morning."

"Yes," I said, thinking this was an odd request made at a strange time.

"In the event you were all going to church, you know."

"May I ask what this is about?"

"I'm afraid Mr. King died."

I gasped.

"I just need to talk to people who spoke with him yesterday to get an idea of a timeline of his movements."

"We'll be here if you'd like to come back at nine," I said.

This was going to be a long day.

I WOKE MY PARENTS, not telling them anything just yet, then Miss Manley to whom I told what I knew. Then I went to the kitchen, making sure the swinging door was closed before calling John.

He answered quickly and I just as quickly asked him what had happened the night before.

"Good morning to you," he said.

"Sorry to have been so abrupt. Good morning, John. Officer Reed was just here and told me that Mr. King is dead."

"Were those his exact words?"

"Yes, except he said he would come back at nine." Something very odd was going on.

"I can come over then if you like."

"All right." I hung up, wondering why the two men were being so vague.

Even though Annie had Saturday and Sunday off that week due to all the work she had put into preparing for houseguests, the accompanying huge meal and a chance to enjoy the Garden Fair, she had baked blueberry muffins before she left. I had volunteered to make the simple bacon and eggs breakfast for us all to my mother's surprise.

"Dear, it didn't occur to me that you were so proficient in the kitchen."

"Thank you, Mother. I will take that as a compliment."

"I saw a very comprehensive basic cookbook the last time I was in the City. Perhaps I should get it for you," she said.

I knew where she was going with this.

"Does Doctor Taylor cook for himself?"

"Oh, yes. I'm not sure what's on the menu each day at his house, but he does prepare dinner for me on Friday evening before we go out to a movie in Adams or listen to the radio."

I turned back to the stove to watch the eggs cook.

"He cooks for *you?*"

I was about to answer that he had been a bachelor a long time before I remembered that hadn't been the case. Instead, I said, "His repertoire is limited but excellent."

She paused, then asked, "Does he have a housekeeper?"

"Someone comes in once a week to clean the house and the office."

I knew in her mind she was imagining us already married and trying to figure out what my responsibilities would be. Wife, nurse, accountant, cook—what else?

In the nick of time, before the questioning became more intense, my father came into the kitchen and asked if he could assist

"Thanks, Dad. The table is set, and the coffee is almost ready, as are the eggs. If you could just take the muffins out to the dining room. I wonder what is keeping Miss Manley?"

"I'll check," my mother said, and no sooner had she stepped into the hall than her hostess appeared at the foot of the stairs.

"So sorry to keep you all waiting," she said, holding a small notebook in her hands.

Looking at the clock in the kitchen, she added, "We'd better sit down before Officer Reed gets here."

A discreet knock on the back door let me know that John had arrived and from the look on his face, he hadn't had breakfast yet.

"Come on, the more the merrier," I said. Perhaps, although I might have been the only one to think there was a pall hanging over us. Then I remembered that while I had told Miss Manley and my parents that Mr. King had died, only she and I wondered if there was something more that Officer Reed hadn't mentioned to me. I carefully examined John's face for a trace of information, and I must have looked stern because he stopped eating.

"What?" he asked.

I recognized that tone at once. He knew more than he either could or wanted to say and we would just have to wait. He helped me clear the table while Miss Manley and my parents went into the sitting room. I looked at him again and got the same response.

"What?"

The doorbell rang. "Would you mind getting that?" I asked him and put the dishes in the sink full of soapy water. Then I went to greet Officer Reed and asked if he would like some coffee, but he said he had just eaten as well. Off we went to the sitting room, and I introduced my parents before he sat down, hat in his lap.

"I'm sorry to tell you that Mr. King, our County Commissioner, was killed last night."

I glanced at John, but he did not meet my eyes.

"I know this is an inconvenient time, Sunday morning and all, just before church, but I wanted to get some idea of where everyone was last evening."

My mother was surprised at the question but deferred to my father for an answer.

"We went to the Mountain Aire for dinner then came home. That's all."

"Before that, I mean."

We looked puzzled. "We were all here," I said.

"From the time the Garden Fair closed for the day until you went out to dinner?"

We looked at one another.

"I took my car into town. I had been rummaging around in the car for my cane and couldn't find it. I thought I might have left it at the Garden Fair near where we were sitting. I walked around the site, but nothing was there. As long as I was in town, I looked for a place to get an afternoon newspaper but couldn't locate one."

"There isn't an afternoon newspaper here," I said, starting to be concerned.

My father chuckled. "Well, I didn't know that, and I spent some time walking about looking for a likely place one would buy a newspaper. But no luck!"

Miss Manley spoke up. "Officer Reed, I didn't see you at the Garden Fair."

"I apologize, ladies, but it was my day off."

"We're not offended that you didn't attend, I just wanted to know if you had witnessed any of the interactions that took place. But I see that could not be possible." She took the notebook that was on the end table and held it up. "I was there, and this morning I carefully pieced together who was where and what was going on. No mean feat considering how many people attended and the comings and goings of everyone. But I was watching Mr. King because, despite having been elected to public office, he could offend some people. Mrs. Proctor, in particular, whom I have known for many years. I wanted to make sure that they didn't have any unpleasantness between them that would leave a bad taste for the rest of us in attendance."

"And were you successful?"

"Not at all," Miss Manley admitted. "I was preoccupied elsewhere, and the clash of personalities was inevitable."

Officer Reed thought for a moment and turned to my father. "And did you find your cane?"

"No, I didn't. I don't know where I left the darned thing."

"I'm afraid we do. It appears to be the murder weapon that killed Mr. King."

Chapter 11

I thought my mother would keel over when she heard those words. Instead, she grabbed my father's hand and protested, "No!"

After a moment where we all looked at each other, she continued. "Someone must have taken his cane. He last saw it in our car and, as he said, it wasn't there when he went into town looking for a newspaper."

My father had regained speech by then. "I didn't even know the man. I first heard his name when he introduced himself from the stage."

"This is a terrible mistake if you are suggesting my father had anything to do with it," I said.

"Please understand, I am making no such insinuation. I'm just telling you that a cane was found near the body and from the multiple head wounds, it appears it is the murder weapon."

"A cane? How do you know it was my father's cane?" I asked.

"I'm afraid it was that distinctive handle," John said. He looked at me for my reaction.

"Oh." My voice was rather small.

"Mr. Burnside, were you planning on going back home today?"

"Yes," my father said, annoyed at the question.

"Inspector Gladstone is coming up from Pittsfield and he would like to talk to you if you can stay for his visit."

My father was not pleased with the idea of leaving later than he had planned but saw no other way out of it.

"Will you still be here in a few hours?"

"We were going to go to church, but, yes, we'll be back afterward," I said. Then I remembered that we were to have Sunday dinner with Glenda. But how long of an interrogation could they have with my father? He had nothing new to share, did not know Mr. King personally and had no reason to harm him.

We trooped off to the church, my parents in their car with Miss Manley while John and I walked.

"I couldn't tell you about the situation before Officer Reed talked to your father," he said.

"Yes, I know. It just seems preposterous that my father would have anything to do with such a thing. He abhors violence."

We nodded to other neighbors making their way to the church, and the bells chimed ten as we walked through the doors. I may have been imagining it, but it seemed as if everyone in the building turned to look as we came in. I clung to John's arm, and he said, "People are just admiring your hat."

That wasn't likely even if it was a fashionable shape and hue. Based on my experience of how information and gossip circulated in West Adams, I knew that most of the congregation had already heard the news of Mr. King's death. It also explained why attendance was greater than usual. I smiled and nodded to those who continued to stare before we took our places in Miss Manley's pew. Nina, the Reverend's wife, sat in the front pew as she did for one service on

Sunday as opposed to the several that she used to attend before the baby was born. Her straight-backed posture gave her husband a clear sign of support for whichever hymns he had chosen and the sermon he would give in about twenty minutes. For some reason, he looked uncomfortable, and I couldn't imagine why. Then, as he approached the pulpit and unfolded the sheet of paper that contained the words he likely had worked over during the previous week, he cleared his throat and began.

"Cain and Abel," he began.

Of all the topics to talk about the day after someone was brutally killed was one that mentioned a homonym of cane. We all knew the Bible story, of course, one brother a herdsman, the other a farmer, both of whom brought offerings to God. Abel's gifts were more appreciated than Cain's, so when they were out in a field, Cain killed his brother. As a child hearing this story, it seemed absurd that someone would kill a sibling over a slight, and it wasn't until I was older that I realized that there could be intense conflicts in a family, especially when one child is favored over another.

Surely Mr. King was not killed because of family conflicts—but I reminded myself that I knew nothing about his personal life. Perhaps he had a secret, jealous brother who showed up and argued with him. More likely people would look to the various people he had trod on and, of course, I thought about Mrs. Proctor. I couldn't turn around and gape at the crowd to see if she was in attendance. I would have to wait until we filed out. I hoped our minister wasn't suggesting that the competition from the gardeners on display the day before could provide a motive. Mr. King was neither a participant nor a judge. And I had not detected any hard feelings from anyone about the outcome of the prizes.

Reverend Lewis seemed to veer off the topic of conflict and jealousy to one of evil and asked, "What is the nature of evil?"

I could see Nina shifting in her seat, which was usually a sign that he was no longer following the sermon he had written, and she didn't know where he was going and where he would land. The direction got a bit vague, and it turned out to be an odd speech that ended with "Love thy neighbor as thyself."

As we filed out, a few of the tea group ladies came up and commented that it was nice to see my parents in attendance and asked how long they were visiting. It should have seemed an innocent enough question, but I couldn't help but think that they were fishing for information. When Inspector Gladstone appeared later in the day and parked his car outside of Miss Manley's house, the town would be abuzz.

John and I walked back home under the maple trees that lined the main street, and I admired the carefully tended gardens along the way. I wondered why some of those neighbors hadn't participated in the garden competition since their efforts would surely have won a ribbon.

"That was the oddest sermon I have ever heard," John said. "And the Reverend has given some doozies."

"Glenda was expecting us for an early dinner, anticipating my parents' departure this afternoon, but now there is even more urgency if Gladstone is about to arrive. I'm not looking forward to it."

"You have nothing to worry about," John said, attempting to reassure me.

"Of course, I do. He will probably suspect my father, which is absurd, and then when he sees me, his antennae will twitch, thinking I had something to do with it."

"Calm down," John said.

"No, that's my line," I said, recalling how many times I had to restrain some of the Garden Fair organizers from panicking over a minor oversight.

In keeping with the strange formality of Sunday dinner, we went to the front door of the younger Manley household next door and could smell roast meat. I was thankful we weren't going to be given

Mrs. Nelson's gruel, as Glenda put it, although I couldn't imagine that's what the woman cooked each day.

"Hello," Glenda said cheerfully, answering the door with Douglas on her hip.

We made our way to the sitting room where Stuart stood waiting to greet us.

"Auntie," he kissed Miss Manley's cheek, then also mine, which was novel, but in the excitement of having so many guests at once, he may have forgotten himself. No sooner had we sat down than the Crompton sisters appeared, their faces tan from being out in the sun, not the awful orange makeup they had on the day before.

"How did the fortune telling go?" I asked and noticed Freya was somewhat embarrassed. So, it must have been she who was kissing or being kissed by Mr. Headley in the tent.

"That was so much fun," Minerva said. "Nobody could think that whoever was dressed in that strange getup could know what would happen in the future, much less the past or present. But after the first moments of sitting down, our customers fell right into the spell of believing the absurd things we said to them."

"Such as?" Glenda asked.

"I usually asked if the letter J meant anything to them. And instead of saying, no, they would think until they could make a connection, as if it were a test or something. One said, 'My dog is named Jojo.'"

"Where did the conversation go with that?" I asked.

"I said some general things about how the dog loved her and other things you might say about a pet without knowing what it was like. Then I suggested that she make sure the gate was latched so he wouldn't get out. And that made her eyes go wide and she said, yes, he would escape with any opportunity. Well, isn't that what dogs do?"

"I guess you can see how those psychics and fortune tellers can pull in gullible people," John said.

"Then if you throw in the 'going on a trip,' that is always an exciting line."

"I thought the usual prediction was meeting a tall, handsome stranger," my mother said, and I could see Freya blushing. Well, *her* prediction came true, all right.

"I had a lot of fun," Minerva said. "I didn't imagine a country fair could be so entertaining. But then, so much about West Adams has been a surprise."

"What do you mean?" Miss Manley asked.

"This peaceful small town and someone gets killed, is what I mean," she said with a bit of a laugh.

That stopped the conversation. Minerva searched our faces to discover what horrible faux pas she had committed.

"Yes, it was dreadful," Miss Manley said. "An inspector from Pittsfield is expected later today to interview some of us about the events of yesterday."

"I'm very sorry if I spoke out of turn. I certainly didn't mean to make light of a tragic situation."

Mrs. Nelson saved the day by appearing in the doorway, letting us know that the meal was ready. I was surprised by her changed appearance from months ago when she was camouflaged by a bulky hooded poncho. Underneath that was a trim woman who had prospered, living in a settled situation with Glenda. The rough living she had experienced at the farm that Farley Dexter owned had once made her look years older than her chronological age. She had decent clothes now, her hair was braided and wound around her head, making her look like a young German woman.

She had outdone herself with the meal of roast pork, parslied potatoes, spinach in cream sauce and a salad of local tomatoes, deep red and dressed only with a bit of salt and pepper. I was looking forward to the blueberry season and in a short while, farmers would bring their corn into town to be sold at the greengrocer's.

We tucked into the meal while Miss Manley took the conversation away from anything that would lead to what happened to Mr. King, instead focusing on the extensive variety of vegetables that had been exhibited at the fair the day before. We all carefully steered away from mentioning the sermon that the Reverend had stumbled through and made it to dessert before being distracted by the doorbell.

Mrs. Nelson came into the dining room with a distressed look on her face and said to Glenda, "That Inspector Gladstone is here."

It was time to face the music.

Chapter 12

"I think we all better go back to my house," Miss Manley said, getting up from the table.

We agreed. Glenda looked crushed that she would not be able to witness first-hand any of the questioning. I saw a glimmer in Stuart's eye that meant he was registering the events soon to be the plot of an upcoming adventure book after he wormed the information out of me later. The Crompton sisters didn't have much of a reaction, not knowing Gladstone's reputation for having a brusque temperament and persistent interrogation style.

As we walked past him out the front door, his face twisted to the side in a knowing smirk.

"Well, I'm not surprised to see you here," he said.

"What do you mean?" my father challenged him.

"If something happens in West Adams, somehow Nurse Burnside can be found in the vicinity."

My mother took my arm as we walked across the lawn to Miss Manley's. "What *did* he mean by that?"

"I'll explain later," I said, hoping she would either forget about it or I could stall her until they left for Pelham. We had already had one uncomfortable conversation about what she thought was my hobby when we were in Boston.

Back to Miss Manley's sitting room, we positioned ourselves in a semi-circle with Gladstone seated in a tall wingback chair, his back to the empty fireplace. He eyed each of us in turn as if we were all suspects.

"Mr. Burnside, I believe," he began in that insufferable sneering tone.

"Yes, that is I," my father replied curtly.

"Please enlighten me. You are a guest here in West Adams this weekend, I understand?"

"You have been correctly informed."

"And staying where?"

"Miss Manley had graciously invited my wife and me to stay this weekend for the Garden Fair."

Gladstone took a small notebook from his breast pocket and scribbled in it with the stub of a pencil.

"Can you tell me your whereabouts yesterday?"

"The whole day?"

"Start when you first left the house."

My father blew out a gust of air. "We were here until midmorning, then drove over to the site."

"Drove?"

"Yes, I had twisted my knee last week and was trying not to walk too much."

"Ah, yes. The cane." More scribbling.

"We got to the fair and sauntered around briefly before sitting down near where mothers and babies were under the trees. There were folding chairs and shade and that's where we stayed for the majority of the event."

"You didn't stroll around the booths?"

"We passed the floral and vegetable displays on our way in. But as I said, my knee has been painful, and I chose to rest it. We had a good view of the stage and could see people coming and going to various amusements, like the bean bag toss and some sort of fishing game set up for children."

"It sounds as if you had an excellent vantage point for observing everyone's actions. Rather like your daughter. Always in the right place at the right time." He scribbled again.

My father looked at me in surprise and alarm, but the expressions left his face as soon as he saw Gladstone's face lift back up.

"And then?"

"As the morning progressed, Agnes brought us something to eat from the refreshment tent and we ate as we sat under the trees."

"Did you talk to anyone?"

"Of course! We chatted with Mrs. Glenda Manley, who was in the fenced-off area with her little boy. Other people came up to us realizing we were not locals and introduced themselves. They were mostly the women of the tea group that Miss Manley organizes."

"Do you remember their names?"

My father gave a huff of exasperation. "Of course not. There were so many, and I didn't anticipate interacting with them again soon. I remembered Mrs. Proctor's name because she was the organizer of the event who came to tell us what a help our daughter had been in putting it together with her. Also, she had previously introduced herself to the crowd, so that cemented it in my mind."

Gladstone was writing furiously to catch up with my father's narrative.

"Did you know Mr. King?"

"I'd never met him before. He introduced himself on the stage and gave a long spiel about his position as County Commissioner and what he had done for the area. When he was done, he mingled with the crowd."

"Was that your last interaction with him?"

"It wasn't an interaction. I merely observed him give a stump speech. We saw him as we stood when the prizes were being awarded. My daughter was one of the judges. Mr. King made a rather crude remark to her as she passed by."

I wished my father hadn't said that, but he was a direct person who valued honesty.

"What did he say?"

"He referred to her as a tall drink of water."

Gladstone scratched his head.

"And he leered at her in a most undignified way."

I was shooting daggers with my eyes at my father, pleading with him to stop providing details, but he held his chin up and ignored me.

"He seemed a most unpleasant person and provoked Mrs. Proctor as well," he added.

"So, I've heard from others," Gladstone said. "Did you confront him about his remark?"

"No, I did not. I did not want to embarrass my daughter or draw attention to it as she was about to announce the winners of the various categories."

"Did you interact with him again during the Fair?"

"No, I did not."

"That's true," my mother said. "I was by his side the entire time." She nodded for emphasis.

"When did you leave the fair site?"

"Not too much later and we came back here."

"Did you return to the fair site?"

"Yes, I did. I had misplaced my cane. I thought I might have left it there and by the time I got there, everything was cleared away. I looked under the trees, thinking I might have placed it on the ground, but couldn't find it."

"So, you came back here?"

"Not immediately. As long as I was out and about, I thought I would search for an afternoon paper."

Gladstone looked askance at my father.

"In the greater New York area, we have many newspapers to choose from. The morning paper is delivered to the house, the **New York Times** is purchased on my train commute into the City, the **Telegraph** I pick up on my way home and the local paper appears on our doorstep in the late afternoon."

The inspector looked as if that was the strangest recitation he had ever heard.

"We're used to many different newspapers, each with their special interest reporting and point of view. I was feeling news starved, to tell the truth."

"There is no afternoon paper in Berkshire County to my knowledge."

"So, I came to find out. But I didn't know that and spent some time searching in the town. There were people out and about, there must have been someone who saw me inquiring."

MURDER AT THE GARDEN FAIR

I didn't like that my father seemed to be clutching at straws at this point and I saw him rub his knee in a defensive motion that Gladstone would surely pick up on.

"What time did you get back here?"

"I think it was less than an hour."

Gladstone stared at my father for a bit and wrote a bit more. I hoped this was the end of things and we could get on with our day.

"Doctor Taylor, let me ask you a few questions."

John looked up sharply.

"You examined the body. What did you determine?"

"I assume you and Officer Reed have already had a conversation about this," was his answer.

"Yes, but I wanted to hear it from the horse's mouth."

"It seems he was struck many times with a wooden object."

"A cane? *The* cane?"

John did not respond.

"Mr. Burnside's cane?"

John was quiet as he looked at me and then my father before responding, "It appears so."

"How do you know?"

Why did he ask if he knew the answer?

"That's the conclusion of Officer Reed because the bloodied cane lay beside the body," John said.

"Where was the body found?"

John hesitated. "In a ditch."

"Where?"

"Behind some maple trees at the edge of the Garden Fair site."

This was the first time I had heard this information, and I was furious that I didn't know it earlier. I stood up abruptly. "You can't possibly imagine that my father, an attorney of impeccable reputation with so mild a temperament that he often serves as a Pro Tem Judge in the Westchester County courts, would beat a man he hardly knows to death?" I was shaking with fury. John pulled me back down onto the loveseat and kept his hand on mine.

"Stranger things have happened," Gladstone said.

"I'm sure you have seen strange things in your line of work," my father said. "But I can assure you, and swear on it, that after I left the fair the first time, I never laid eyes on that man again." I loved that his chin jutted out at this statement, challenging Gladstone to prove otherwise.

Gladstone then asked John about his movements, which had been observed by many people, and he had the obvious alibi of being with me most of the time. Except when he dropped me off at Miss Manley's and I had a nap. He said that he went home, began to read a medical journal and fell asleep as well.

Miss Manley related how she had been at the site beginning early in the morning, returning home briefly to cut her roses for the exhibit and then gone back to the Garden Fair. Like all of the women who participated in putting the fair together, she was busy the entire time, making sure the children's games were set up, relieving the women in the refreshment tent and finally coming out to sit with my parents before the awarding of the prizes.

"Did you know Mr. King?" Gladstone asked.

"Of course, I knew him. He is president of the Adams Bank. We don't have a bank in West Adams so we need to go to the other town for financial transactions. I have seen him from time to time going into his office at the rear of the bank."

"That's all?"

"Of course not." She pursed her lips at his question. "You and I know that he is a County Commissioner so that those of us who attend public meetings see him there. That's practically the entire town."

For once, he may have realized how ridiculous this interrogation was because he kept his head down, wrote more and then turned the page. What I wouldn't have given to see his notes.

"And now we come to Miss Burnside."

I didn't like his tone one bit. He made it sound like I was the most likely suspect! Not giving an inch, I smiled briefly in his direction.

"How do you know Mr. King?"

"I had never seen him before yesterday."

"Not even at the bank in Adams? I thought everybody around here banked there."

"I have gone there for some transactions. Deposits, and so forth. But if I had seen him in the bank, I wouldn't have known who he was."

"Oh, come now. Miss Manley said anyone who attended public meetings would know who he was," Gladstone said.

"I've only lived here a year, Inspector. Since I do not own property or pay taxes here, I have no interest in attending the County meetings. As a relative newcomer, I wouldn't be familiar with the local issues that concerned the neighbors. What little I know, I've heard from Miss Manley's reports afterward or from the tea group's conversations."

"Aha! The tea group. Now we come to Mrs. Proctor. How well do you know her?"

"I know her socially through the tea group, that's all."

"And do you know that she intends to run for the County Commissioner position? The one now vacated by the death of Mr. King?"

"Hold on," my father interrupted. "My daughter is not on the witness stand and you are not the prosecutor. She has said how she knows the woman. Why are you making it appear that Agnes knows more than she has already said?"

"I beg your pardon. I had forgotten that you were an attorney."

"We are not in a courtroom," my father said sternly. "I do not like your tone."

To break the tension, I spoke up. "I also assisted Mrs. Proctor in some of the organizing chores for the Garden Fair. We have interacted in that capacity over the past few weeks. That's all." I had no intention of telling him that I attended a campaign committee meeting of hers. There was no telling where he would go with that information.

Chapter 13

A few more questions about my whereabouts followed and then Gladstone seemed to run out of steam. It was a good thing because my father was obviously in pain, having been seated for so long, and his patience was wearing thin.

A sigh of relief swept over us all after Gladstone left, and I peeked between the curtains in the dining room to see if he was going back to Glenda's to grill them. But he got in his car and left, whether to chat with Officer Reed or back to Pittsfield, I couldn't be certain. I went back to Glenda's and invited her over to our place—with the dessert, of course—so we'd have coffee and cake before my parents left for home.

"What was it like?" she asked me as we crossed the back gardens to our kitchen door. Stuart hurried to catch up and overhear the conversation.

"The usual. He thinks he will impress everyone by giving them a third degree. By the way, Stuart. What are the first and second degree?"

"What an intriguing question! I don't know, never having been 'grilled,' as you put it, by the police, or even arrested, for that matter. But it would make for an excellent book title: The First, the Second and the Third Degree."

"Maybe that's three books, each with its own title," I suggested.

"That's even better. A suspenseful build-up to the third in the series. Aggie, you should give up the blood and gore and work for me creating fictional blood and gore."

"Thank you for the offer, Stuart, but seeing the pace at which the Crompton sisters work, I prefer what I am doing. Yours might be the more entertaining profession—there's nothing wrong with that, but mine has a definite impact on peoples' lives." I realized that sounded rather pompous, but I didn't care.

Everyone was pleased with the resumption of Sunday dinner being dessert at Miss Manley's, and sick of Gladstone's clumsy questioning, we tacitly made a pact not to discuss it further despite Stuart's and Glenda's curiosity.

IT WASN'T until the next morning that we learned Inspector Gladstone had spent the remainder of the afternoon at the Proctors' home, this time with Officer Reed in tow, interviewing husband and wife separately. I couldn't imagine that it went well, and Annie confirmed that my intuition was correct. How she knew, I couldn't say, but with all the visiting back and forth among households and interactions at the shops on the main street, information buzzed along rapidly. Having seen Mrs. Proctor, who did not bear fools easily, in action with those who slowed her down or impeded her wishes, I wished I had been a fly on the wall. Let Gladstone go back to Pittsfield and lick his wounds.

"Did you know that he had even talked to Mrs. Nelson?" Annie asked, bent over the sink scrubbing at something.

"How odd. Whatever for?"

"Somehow he found out that neither she nor Joanna and the baby had attended the Garden Fair."

"That might stand as a crime as far as the tea group is concerned but so what?"

Annie lowered her voice, although there was no one there to overhear us. "I know the woman has had a rough life, but I think there is more to her than meets the eye."

"Whatever are you doing?" I asked her as she attacked something with a scrub brush.

"Mrs. Nelson was trying to get this stain off Glenda's blouse, you know, the one that one of the Cromptons wore at the fair. I don't know what it's made of, but nothing either she or I have tried will get it out. I give up."

"It looks like brown shoe polish," I said.

"It's that awful makeup they put on for the fortune-telling business."

Something rang a bell, but I couldn't remember if it was something I had heard or something I had seen.

Annie rinsed it with water and sighed at her failure but resumed talking.

"She has been very vague about a lot of things, such as how she and Joanna came to be up at the farm working for Mr. Dexter, for instance." She nodded her head in a way that told me she could imagine many more interesting scenarios in the Nelsons' past than I had.

"She told me he had advertised for people to work on a farm in the newspaper when she lived in Hartford, that her husband had left and she had no money and no job."

"She's stuck by that story with me, too. But who is little Rosalie's father, I'd like to know?" She was referring to Joanna's baby, who was born not too long after they had moved into the community.

"She has always been cautious about saying anything about it," I said, picking up a piece of toast and biting off a corner.

"Anyway, what Mrs. Nelson told Inspector Gladstone was that because she was relatively new to the town and it was her day off, she chose not to attend the Garden Fair. That's true. But I happen to know that she, Joanna and the baby went up to the farm." She smiled at knowing much more than I ever would about the comings and goings of the townsfolk.

As usual, the mailman in Adams came into the office to hand me the mail rather than leave it in the box outside the front door. I didn't know if he did this with all of the professional and commercial customers, but it was always a pleasure to see his beaming smile and pick up some tidbit of local gossip. He surprised me with a good one that day.

"Well, if it isn't the snake charmer's assistant!" he said with a laugh.

Thankfully, no one else was in the reception area at the time or there would have been some explaining to do.

"I didn't see you there," I said.

"No, couldn't make it. But I heard it was very funny."

I wondered what he had heard. Snake charmer sounded as if I had been dressed in some exotic outfit, gyrating with a live animal coiled around my neck, instead of my usual sedate nurse's uniform, cap and all.

Overhearing the conversation, John put his head out of his office. "You should have been there. We brought down the house."

"Don't be surprised if the Elks, the Moose and the local Rotary Clubs call you for an engagement."

"I hope not. That's all the performance material we have. I don't have time to develop a vaudeville routine." He had taken the mailman's comments, which I thought were teasing, to be serious. At least, I hoped he was teasing.

"There you go," he said, handing me a pile of letters and a journal. "I hear Doctor Mitchell is thinking about selling the place."

"That's what I hear, too," John said.

"He still gets mail to this address, so I keep it for when I stop by toward the end of my route and we chat. I hope you get to stay here. It's been a doctor's office for a long time." He touched the brim of his hat as he left.

"Aggie, I hope this doesn't sound crass, but if Mr. King is no longer bank president then someone else surely oversees loan applications. Perhaps I should try again."

"It's not crass, just practical. Only, who is that? The assistant who said, 'If it were up to me....'?"

"I'll give a call over there later and see if they have assigned responsibility to someone else."

"Good idea."

He stood there a moment and then said, "I don't know if I told you this but the oddest thing about Mr. King's death was the presence of what looked like shoe polish on the side of his head, his collar and the cane."

"Did Officer Reed notice?"

"Yes, whether he told Gladstone or not, I'm not sure. That's why the assumption is that a man committed the crime. Brown shoe polish."

"Are you sure it wasn't something else, like dried blood?"

"No, it had that greasy texture—it wasn't dried."

"That is very odd."

"The entire thing is very odd."

He returned to his office, and I began to open the mail. A short while later, the front door opened, and Freya Crompton came in haltingly. At first, I thought she was being cautious but then saw that walking was painful, and I asked if she would like to sit down.

"Oh, no, not yet," she answered with an odd expression on her face. "I'd like to see the doctor. It's an emergency."

"Of course," I said, moving swiftly to get him from his office where he sat reading.

"Right this way," I said, leading her into the exam room.

She stood next to the chair where patients usually sat and waited until he came in. She looked from him to me, inhaled deeply and said, "I believe I have poison ivy."

I glanced down at her hands and didn't notice a rash and looking back at her face, she was blushing deeply.

"I'm afraid I was in the woods and decided to relieve myself in nature rather than walking back to the house."

"Ouch," John said. "We'll take a look. Nurse, could you help her into a gown? I'll be back in a few minutes."

We stepped to the far corner of the room where there was a screen. She took off her thin rayon dress and folded it carefully on the bench, then removed her slip and I could see the rash was extensive, from the back of her thighs visibly red through the fabric of her underwear. Even on the back of her arms. Ouch, indeed.

"The itching is driving me crazy," she said.

I held the gown open for her to put her arms through and assisted her to the table, face down then went to get John. By the twisted grimace I made, he knew exactly what this was about.

"Oh, my," he said. "You have a spectacular case."

"Can you put me to sleep for a few days until this goes away?" she asked.

John exhaled. "I'm afraid I cannot. Let's turn you over. Any on the front side?"

She turned carefully, wincing as she moved. "I don't think so."

He examined her skin and agreed.

"There's not much that can be done. Cold compresses, oatmeal bath and calamine lotion can all sooth the irritation, but the itching won't stop until the blisters go down."

Her shoulders slumped.

"It might take as long as two weeks."

"The wages of sin," she said. "I guess I'll get a nice soft pillow to sit on and do my best."

"There's no prescription but I'll write down the things you can get from the pharmacy."

"Thank you."

"Do you need help getting dressed?" I asked, but she shook her head. It was going to be a miserable two weeks. I hadn't had poison ivy in years but remembered well how insanely itchy it was, a real torment. I wondered if her partner was suffering, too, before letting my mind wander to who that might be.

Chapter 14

It was difficult to concentrate that afternoon back in West Adams since the tea group was set to meet to discuss the success of the Garden Fair. As Annie prepared lunch, she told me that many more people than Mr. and Mrs. Proctor and we had been interviewed. Her source was not from her vast network of friends and neighbors but Officer Reed, whom she now referred to as Tom, letting slip information that he probably should have kept to himself. But although he felt he needed to satisfy her curiosity, he never stooped to the level of telling her the word-for-word results of the interviews that Gladstone conducted.

"I imagine Mrs. Proctor was not pleased to be the center of attention in this sad drama," I said.

"Oh, no. Her husband is a mild-mannered man and, as you know, she can be a real firecracker. For once, I'm sorry that I won't be around for the tea group. I would like to know what she tells you all about it." At this, she looked pointedly at me.

"Of course. I'll tell you tomorrow morning when you get here."

She smiled. "And I made your favorite bar cookies," she added.

That was the delight of the tea group meetings. Annie baked all morning for the afternoon event. In return, she was done with work after lunch and had a nice half-day to herself—probably doing cooking and baking for her parents and younger siblings, the bane of being the oldest female child in the family. I had often wondered why she wasn't married already. The fate of the caretaker child was usually to get married as soon as legally possible. Annie was just a bit older than I and had worked out of the house since leaving high school. Maybe the impending wedding of Sam and Elsie was making her think twice about her future.

I looked at my watch. "I've got to go. I'll be all ears and give you the scoop!" I hurried next door to John's home office and saw three people in the reception area.

"Sorry, I'll get the doctor," I said.

"He's already in the exam room with someone," Mrs. Harris said. "No snake, though." She giggled at her joke, and I realized that we were going to live with those jokes for a long time.

JOHN ALWAYS ALLOWED me to leave early on tea group afternoons so I could participate in the 'information sharing,' as he put it. In reality, he was just as interested in the town's gossip but would not admit it, and he couldn't participate in it since he knew too much personal information about everyone.

The women were just settling themselves in Miss Manley's sitting room as I came across the back garden and saw them through the French windows. I couldn't wait to hear how much money the Garden Fair earned, and I hoped that morbid curiosity about Mr. King's death wouldn't cast a shadow over the success of their efforts. I took off my cap and slid into a chair near the entry from the hall, noticing that the group had grown since the last meeting.

"How nice to see so many of you here," Mrs. Proctor began. Although it was Miss Manley's group and it took place in Miss Manley's house, Mrs. Proctor seemed to have taken over.

"What an extraordinary weekend of highs and lows," she began. "The Garden Fair was a tremendous success. But then there was the tragedy of the passing of Mr. King."

She made it sound as if he had died in his sleep, but her phrasing had everyone shaking their heads sadly.

"That was unfortunate," Miss Olsen said. Then, with a gleam in her eye, she stated, "But now Mrs. Proctor is our County Commissioner." She clapped and many applauded.

"No, Miss Olsen," her mentor said. "There is still an election to be had. We're not there yet."

"But…," Miss Olsen stammered. She looked around the room for confirmation that she had been correct.

"The existing Commissioners can appoint someone to finish out his term and then with the election, someone will take that position."

Miss Olsen's shoulders slumped.

"Perhaps they won't appoint anyone," Mrs. Rockmore suggested.

"That's possible, but then Mr. Headley and Mr. Campbell will have to agree on everything or there will always be one vote against one vote. That's why there are an odd number of Commissioners."

"Odd, I'll say," someone murmured.

"It seems to me that the three of them never disagreed on much," Miss Manley said. "According to their votes."

"Yes, I noticed that, too. It's almost as if they decided to take the pie and divide it equally amongst themselves. 'I'll scratch your back, et cetera.'" Mrs. Proctor added. "Who knows what deals those three cooked up? But we should not be speaking ill of the deceased," she said in a solemn tone, although she had already done so.

Taking a deep breath, she resumed her leadership tone. "Now to the reports from the committee chairs."

I was unaware that each person who had been assigned a committee was expected to speak about what went well and what problems there were to prevent mishaps in the future.

There could have been more food and, since that was a source of income, it was suggested that a larger variety be provided next year. I was called on next and said that the flyers posted in Adams and the guests from the Mountain Aire swelled the attendance significantly. The entertainment sign-up lists were full and although some of the performances were unusual—here I thought but did not say the spoon playing or the strange whistling farmer—everyone seemed to enjoy themselves.

"The doctor and the snake were so funny!" Miss Ballantine said. Everyone agreed and I allowed myself to blush.

After the committees had finished reporting, Mrs. Proctor read out the revenue, and here there was a big whoop from everyone as the expenses were modest. I quickly calculated the income that she pronounced with flair. There were much clapping and many happy voices in the room and I had to admit it was quite an achievement from that group of amateurs in a small town.

As the group began to break up sometime later, Miss Olsen looked very distressed.

"What's the matter?" I asked as she passed me in the hallway.

"Mrs. Proctor said if she were elected, she would hire me as her assistant."

"There, there," Mrs. Proctor said, patting her protégée on the back. "It will be the second thing I do. The first thing is to make sure that insufferable Inspector Gladstone is fired."

Everyone who stood nearby was silent, waiting for more, and she did not disappoint.

"Imagine—he came to our house on a Sunday and interrogated my husband and me like common criminals. He wouldn't allow us to be in the same room together, as if we had concocted alibis or had some secret signals to give the other if the wrong answer were made."

"I don't like his attitude at all, either," I said. I probably had more interactions with him than anyone present, but I hesitated to say more just then.

"He is supposed to be a servant of the people, not the Grand Inquisitor. He'll be singing a different tune soon enough." She nodded her head for emphasis, and those of us still standing like marionettes pulled by a collective string did the same.

"If Mr. Headley and Mr. Campbell don't stand up for him," I murmured as the women left. It occurred to me at the same time that Gladstone worked for the Pittsfield Police Department, not the County Sheriff, and the Commissioners likely didn't have the authority to fire him in any case. If that were true, and Mrs. Proctor won the seat, she would find out soon enough.

Once the house was cleared, Nina asked me to step outside for a moment. When we got into the back garden, away from anyone possibly hearing us, she began, "Did you know that Commissioner Headley spoke to Robert recently?"

"We were out here enjoying the evening air and he approached from the back path, asking if he had got the right directions to your house."

"I don't feel I am revealing a confidence in telling you that he asked Robert to let Joanna go."

"What? Why?"

"He said that it looked bad for the community for a minister to be harboring a woman of ill repute."

"What business was it of his?"

"Exactly. But you know Robert. He was very diplomatic and, of course, referred to Biblical texts about forgiveness, not throwing the first stone and so forth. Their chat wasn't very long and I couldn't understand his purpose in coming."

I had all kinds of thoughts about why he might have made that visit but said nothing. Could he be Rosalie's father? That didn't seem possible since Joanna was pregnant when she came to West Adams. Unless they knew each other beforehand.

"And then, on Saturday morning, Mr. King showed up with the same request. Only this time, Joanna was in the next room and overheard part of the conversation. I was just about to get Eleanor to take her to the Garden Fair when I heard Joanna crying and asked what had happened. She said she was sorry to have caused so much trouble for us, she was going up to the farm with Rosalie and her mother for the day but would be back in the evening to pack her things."

"I'm sure you tried to dissuade her," I said.

"Of course, but I was already running late. I made her promise that she would not take any sudden action and come back so we could discuss it. She agreed. You know she is sometimes such a passive person, it breaks my heart that she doesn't stand up for herself more."

"Well, she came back, didn't she?"

"I don't know if just being away for the day with her mother and the baby helped her get some perspective or being on that familiar land, but she listened to what Robert and I had to say and agreed to stay. It was odd. It seemed like she had already made up her mind and was just being polite in listening to our boring harangue. I just had to share this with somebody." Nina put her hand on my arm. "Thank you."

What was the attraction of the farm, anyway? It was once a working farmstead that fell into disrepair after the former owner died, then Farley Dexter bought it, intending to turn it into a health farm, so he said. In reality, he had some strange scheme of growing mushrooms and fungi in the underground tunnels on the property for commercial sale and some for what he called 'medicinal' purposes. Joanna and her mother had lived in primitive conditions there along with some others who had continued to expand the enterprise by additional excavation or harvesting. The County deemed the property unsafe, so the operations had to cease, although they allowed Dexter to continue living in the dilapidated house.

Was the farm a place of respite for Joanna and her mother despite the nasty living conditions? Or was she attached to one of the workers there? I couldn't for a moment think that she and Dexter had any sort of interest in one another, but I did wonder who the father of the fair Rosalie was and why Joanna was silent about the baby's paternity.

It wasn't until the next morning that I learned from Annie that Inspector Gladstone had interviewed both Joanna and her mother, which seemed ridiculous to me. These two women had been through a lot in their lives. Abandonment, loss of home and income, then transplanted to a rural farm to work underground like gnomes, an unexpected pregnancy with complications of preeclampsia, then escaping homelessness again thanks to the soft hearts of Reverend Lewis and Nina, who took in the young mother and child, and Glenda, who hired Mrs. Nelson.

Nina had told me about the grievances either of the Nelsons could have had with Mr. King, but surely Inspector Gladstone was not privy to that information. Rather, I suspected that he, much like Mr. Headley and Mr. King, was intent on punishing Joanna as the 'fallen woman,' somehow corrupting the town and environs. They were easy targets—without community stature, money or anywhere else to go. This onslaught of prejudice against the two of them made me angry on their behalf, and I was determined to protect them. It was awful that women had to endure the sniggering assumptions of men when, from what I had observed, both Headley and King were no angels, despite what Freya thought. Mr. King was that avuncular-looking type with the leering remarks—was there more? The handsome Headley had had his hands all over Freya in the fortune-telling tent, at least I thought it was Freya. Whichever sister it was, she did not seem to be resisting, but I knew he was a married man with a reputation to protect. Why he chose to pick on her, I couldn't imagine.

Chapter 15

Who should waltz into the Adams office the next day but Mr. Headley. He was still just as handsome and full of himself, although he introduced himself as Mr. Smith.

Really. How original.

I pretended not to recognize him, and he certainly couldn't have remembered me from the time he asked directions from a group of people in a dark garden or fleetingly at the Garden Fair with so many others in attendance. I had him fill out a form and I noticed he didn't indicate he was from Pittsfield. When it came time for the examination, he asked to see John alone. I busied myself with sorting through the mail, but my mind was whirling with suspicion.

Only twenty minutes later, 'Mr. Smith' came out of the exam room, thanked John and asked me if he could settle the bill then.

Very few people asked that.

I wrote out an invoice, he looked at it and dug into his pocket and pulled out cash.

"Thank you," and he was gone.

John came out of the exam room, and I had two words for him: "Poison ivy?"

His mouth dropped open.

"Mr. Headley has been a busy man, I would say." I returned to my paperwork.

"Ah, I thought he looked familiar. And I made a vow of confidentiality. I can neither confirm nor deny your assumption."

I made that zipper motion across my mouth, which got a laugh.

On our way back to West Adams at noon we saw the familiar sight of a man striding along the sidewalk, cloak billowing out behind him. Farley Dexter. Only it wasn't. It was a young, clean-shaven man with short hair.

"It *is* Farley Dexter," I said to John.

"What an incredible change. He's almost unrecognizable."

I craned my neck to stare as we passed him, intent on his thoughts.

It wasn't until after work that day that an unusual explanation came my way. Miss Manley wasn't home when I entered the kitchen, fragrant with bread baking, and asked Annie where she might be.

"Mrs. Lewis came by some time ago and asked her to assist with something important."

I shrugged it off and went upstairs to change out of my uniform. The thought occurred to me that perhaps it was time to wear street clothes to work instead of grappling with the white stockings, shoes and endless starching and ironing of the uniforms. I would ask John if he minded if my attire was professional-looking. Now dressed in slacks and a shirt, I was ready to have a large glass of lemonade.

Miss Manley had come into the kitchen and was removing her hat. That was odd. She put on a hat to go next door? I'm sure my head tilted to the side in curiosity the way hers often did, and she smiled at the familiar gesture.

"I won't ask you two to sit down," she said to Annie and me, "but I certainly need to."

With that, her hat in her lap, she looked from one of us to the other.

"You'll never imagine where I've been."

"We know where you've been, but I am dying to know why." Annie wiped her hands on a dish towel and waited.

"I was just one of the witnesses at a wedding."

"What?" Annie and I said at once.

"Joanna just got married."

"To whom?" we both said.

"Mr. Farley Dexter."

We were shocked into silence, and both of us sat down waiting for the details.

"That's why Mrs. Lewis came to get me. They needed another witness."

"Did they get married in the church?"

"No, in the Reverend's study, with Mrs. Lewis, me and little Rosalie as witnesses but, of

course, she legally doesn't count as one."

"Gosh!" was all I could muster.

"Was it sudden like?" Annie asked.

"They had planned it for some time and got the license beforehand."

"Mrs. Nelson wasn't there?" I asked.

"I got the impression from Mrs. Lewis that the bride's mother was not at all pleased by the impending event."

"I'll ask the obvious: is he the father of the baby?"

Miss Manley took a deep breath and exhaled. "I didn't know the young man at all before

and I'm not sure I do now, but he seems to have had some sort of change of heart. At the start of the ceremony, he said he had amends to make and went into a long speech about his selfish life and actions, by which time Joanna was weeping uncontrollably and I was afraid they would halt the entire thing. Instead, he took a large handkerchief out of his pocket and gently wiped the tears from her face."

"Oh, how romantic!" Annie said, clutching her hands together under her chin like a silent movie actress.

"It must have been very touching," I added. The man had been an enigma to me before, and this current behavior did little to enlighten me.

"Is she going to stay with them or go up to the farm?" Annie asked.

"I got the impression that he's trying to fix it up as a home rather than the strange business he had previously planned."

Annie looked perplexed. "And they'll be farmers?"

I could hardly imagine how that would work out.

"I get the impression he has some kind of trust fund that he lives off."

"It would explain how he was able to purchase the farm in the first place. But it doesn't mean he can figure out how to make money out of it. I can't see him getting up at the crack of dawn to milk the cows and feed the chickens."

Annie laughed loudly at the picture I had painted.

"And the poor house is practically falling around him."

"Oh, dear. Well, young love finds a way, I suppose."

"I wonder if the County will go ahead and condemn the property, now that Mr. King is not pushing to have it done?" Annie asked.

I looked at Miss Manley. "Mrs. Proctor said Mr. King had bought property next to the bridge for a low price and suggested that he would probably get the County to fund its repair. I wonder if he had his eye on Dexter's farm, too. Once it was condemned and the value plummeted, he could have bought it for a song. Of course, I don't know if that was his intention."

"It seems like there were a lot of people whom he stepped on or tried to step over. Gladstone has his hands full with this case. If he lasts that long."

They both looked at me with alarm.

"That is not a threat on my part. Mrs. Proctor intends to see he is no longer around if she is elected. She was very vocal about it."

Miss Manley tutted at hearing that. "I wish this entire business were over with. Glenda told me that the Inspector had a one-on-one meeting with Mrs. Nelson, who was furious after the interview."

"He seems to have that effect on most people."

"Glenda said he spoke to the Crompton sisters, as well."

"That's ridiculous," I said. "They are new to town, they didn't even know Mr. King." Then it occurred to me that 'new to town' didn't slow down Freya's knowing Mr. Headley in short order. I firmly believed that Gladstone didn't have any idea whom he was looking for or any clue about a motive. All he knew was that Mr. King was an important man, prone to throwing his weight around, a bit too quick with his comments—and very dead.

Chapter 16

One of the perks of the expansion of John's practice was the contract he had secured with the Mountain Aire Hotel for any guests who needed medical attention. For people on vacation, this meant a host of ailments that didn't need a doctor, but we were ready to oblige, as were the owners, the Fosters, for the sake of keeping the clientele happy. It seemed a little silly to me to drive over there to diagnose a sunburn—which should have been self-evident to the inflamed person who had summoned us—but the calm tones of John Taylor and the soothing lotions he provided seemed to reassure everyone. There were complaints about mosquito bites, strained muscles from hiking and from time to time a sudden, short-lived fever.

Cash Ridley had become one of John's regular patients since the summer before and, because he had what he thought was a heart attack scare, wanted to see a doctor regularly to make sure he was in the best of health. He oversaw a large business empire that had begun with fitting out households with stainless steel sinks and appliances, then moved into large-scale manufacturing for the automobile industry. He was, as they say, filthy rich. And lived like it.

As the summer before, he rented an entire floor of the hotel: a bedroom for himself, one for his secretary, another for an assistant and a large living area with a spectacular view of the mountains where they worked. It was there that we made our usual visits to check on Cash's heart, blood pressure and general health, which was for the most part excellent.

We were welcomed heartily by Bernard, his assistant and one-time son-in-law, and got a smile and a wave from Catherine, seated at a typewriter at the far end of the room, who then got up to greet us. After John was ushered into Cash's bedroom for the examination and the door was closed, I sat with them on the sofa.

"I heard about that dreadful death in Adams," she said.

"Yes, and the body was found adjacent to the Garden Fair's grounds, as well. I hope it doesn't scare people away from the event next year as a result," I said. "I meant to find you both but was caught up in the frantic last-minute details that those events require."

"It was a lovely event and so nice to get away from work for a day," Catherine said.

It hadn't occurred to me that, since they were here for weeks on end, Cash probably wondered why anyone would want to take time off.

"I see your neighbor Roger Lewis has taken up the position as the man on the clay court again. He enjoys being one of a foursome, as necessary. Just last week, Mr. Headley and Miss Crompton were in search of two more and it happened to suit my schedule."

My ears perked up at this. "I believe he lives in Pittsfield but likes to come up here for a change." That comment was entirely made up as I knew nothing of his habits except an attraction for Freya.

Catherine laughed. "Roger is a dear. He seems to fall in love a little bit with every woman he encounters."

"I noticed that. It's a good thing he will be attending an all-male school in the fall."

"That won't stop him. That's all the boys talk about. I should know," Bernard said.

We chatted until the door opened and the beaming face of Cash told us that he had once again been pronounced in excellent health.

"Dreadful thing about that King fellow," he said, suddenly solemn.

I worried that perhaps the word had got around that my father's cane was the murder weapon, but judging from the matter-of-fact conversation that followed, apparently not.

"I shouldn't say this, but he impressed me as a rather slick person."

"In what way?" John asked.

"Trying a little too hard, a typical politician. Not my type at all."

I was glad that Cash, who was known for sizing people up quickly, had the same sense of the man that I had. He invited us to stay for lunch, but there were patients' appointments to be kept for the afternoon, and lunch with Cash would be a two-hour event.

We drove into Adams to the strange sight of Farley Dexter standing in front of the post office waving papers at people who passed. John slowed down and he spotted us. He trotted to the open driver's side window.

"Stop corruption at its heart! Elect an honest man!"

He thrust a half-page flyer into John's hand with a smile. "I'm running for County Commissioner," he said.

I was too shocked to say anything and just smiled as John handed me the paper and we pulled slowly away.

"What in heaven's name is he up to now?" he asked. "First a health farm, then a mushroom farm, then he gets married, now he wants to run for public office? Is he even a legal resident, I wonder?"

He stopped the car as Mrs. Proctor was storming across the street, intent on challenging Dexter from the look on her face. She saw us and decided to share her fury.

"That man is insane! He has no business running for Commissioner here. Let him go back to New York City and try his fortunes there. Ha—he thinks it will be easy to dupe all of us country bumpkins. I'll bet he'll be handing out dollar bills soon to buy votes. And that scandalous relationship with the Nelson girl. That ought to disqualify him immediately." She stopped to take a breath.

I desperately wanted to ask her to calm down but knew that would be tossing kerosene on a blazing fire, so I kept silent, as did John.

"He stole my campaign platform, as well! And just to copy me, he sneaked into the County Recorder's office to overhear what information I requested. I'm the one who originally pointed out the corrupt dealings of Mr. King, not Farley Dexter. Who knows if the other Commissioners are in on it, too? Or maybe they put Dexter up to this campaign notion, hoping to paint the both of us with the brush of 'crackpot.' And another thing, I'm sure it's illegal to electioneer on post office property." She continued in this vein as she moved past us and toward the offending party who had attracted a lot of attention by this time.

John and I both turned around to see her barreling down the street in Dexter's direction as if she would push him off the sidewalk, which almost happened. He was so shocked by her appearance, her finger-pointing, fist-shaking tirade, which we could not hear but see as if in pantomime, that he tripped as he moved back and landed on his behind. The small crowd that had assembled were at first quiet then burst into laughter, whether at her ability to cow a grown man or his inelegant landing.

In any case, she recovered from her outburst nicely, hands on hips and smiling to the gathering as if she had summoned them before making what looked like an impromptu campaign speech that ended with a round of applause from her admirers.

"Gosh!" I said as we turned forward. "That woman is a powerhouse. She is not going to be stopped by anyone."

Word of the incident must have reached far and wide by the next day. First, Dexter was no longer seen trying to hand out campaign flyers anywhere, unless he went door to door at neighboring farms. Second, the elusive Jesse Campbell, the County Commissioner from District 3 was seen coming into West Adams and parked very obviously in front of the Proctors' house. Since very few people knew what he looked like, not much notice was taken of this clandestine visit. Not too many hours later, the more recognizable Mr. Headley, driving slowly through town as though he didn't know where he was going but doing his best to make his presence known to all who observed, parked in front of the Proctors' house. His car was there a good hour.

For the astute observers who reported the sightings, the verbal exchanges and speculations were intense, and telephones rang throughout West Adams for the rest of the day. I only heard of this later, when I got back from work and Annie was practically hopping up and down with excitement.

"You'll never guess."

Miss Manley had come into the kitchen with a resigned expression on her face.

"What now?" I asked.

"The Commissioners want to appoint Mrs. Proctor! Can you imagine?"

I looked at Miss Manley. "Interesting. Has she agreed?"

Annie looked at me as if I had asked if someone would refuse a bag of gold presented to them. "Well, I don't know. But I can't imagine that she would say no at this point." She looked from Miss Manley to me, not understanding why I had asked the question.

"If she agrees, then she can hardly keep saying Mr. King was corrupt. Because if he was corrupt, why didn't the other two know about it? And if they did know about it, shouldn't they be painted with the same brush?" I asked.

"But she doesn't have to campaign now," Annie said.

"She may have the appointment to fill out the rest of Mr. King's term, but she still has to run for the elected position in the fall," Miss Manley explained. "She'll be in a stronger position than any opponent, but nobody knows if she will have any opposition."

"Mrs. Proctor may have won round one with Farley Dexter, but he may not give up so easily," I said.

Chapter 17

Indeed, he didn't. The next morning, as we were leaving Adams, we spotted him handing out flyers in front of the bank and now holding a clipboard in his hand that he passed to those who would sign it.

"Why is he gathering signatures?" I asked John. "I'm surprised he is so well organized."

"Maybe he is putting together a petition to oust one or all of the Commissioners."

"Oh, dear. Why does there have to be so much commotion all the time?"

He saw John's car approach and flagged him down.

"Good morning, good citizens," he said cheerfully. I don't think I had ever seen him smile before.

"What do you have there?" John asked.

"I'm sure you have heard the rumbling and grumblings about the County Commissioners—what they do and what they don't do. Mrs. Proctor may have run me out of West Adams, but more people live here, and they'll carry the district's vote."

"Did you know that the remaining Commissioners intend to appoint her to fill out Mr. King's term?" John asked.

Dexter's face fell but he recovered quickly. "So that's the gambit! Just as she is homing in on their corrupt behavior, they silence her with the reward of the seat! Brilliant. It's a classic political maneuver to co-opt the opposition. I'm surprised she was so easily bought off."

"It might do you well, as a campaign strategy, to tone down the rhetoric," John said. "No one has proven any corruption…."

"Yet!"

"Nor has anyone suggested Mrs. Proctor was bought off. We don't even know if she has accepted their offer." As ever, John was being reasonable.

Dexter was having none of it and went off on a tangent about big corporations gobbling up small-town America, the demise of unions and the horror of capitalism. Someone came up to him and asked what he was giving away, which allowed us to make our escape.

"He has interesting ideas, but I'm not sure that the bread-and-butter issues of this part of Berkshire County are unions and capitalism," John said as he parked the car.

"And it doesn't look like anybody has been eager to gobble up West Adams, either. Well, maybe his sentiments will play to the public. Who knows?"

When I got to the office in West Adams after lunch, John had already brought in the mail, and that day's portion was sizeable. He was still in the kitchen finishing his sandwich as I began to sort through the hand-addressed envelopes that contained cash and change for services rendered. There was a larger, thin one with a typed address, unusual to see from our patients, and I opened it and gasped. It was a check for $5,000. I looked at the address on the check and it was the American Life Insurance Company.

"John!" I called with some urgency as I went through the door from the office to his kitchen. He was just rinsing a plate in the sink and turned to see what the matter was.

"There's this huge check!" I said, holding it out for him to see.

He took it in his hand and stared at it. "There must be some mistake."

I heard someone come into the reception area and call out to see if anyone was in.

"Just a minute," I responded to the voice, walking briskly back out.

It was Mrs. Proctor. I hoped she wasn't there to rope me into some job like campaign manager, but it was more benign.

"I don't have an appointment, but I was wondering if I could see the doctor?"

"Of course, let me just get him." I scooted back to the door to his kitchen, knocked and walked in to see him looking puzzled.

"I have no idea what this is. I'm not the only John Taylor in the world. Some mix-up. I'll call them later."

Although Mrs. Proctor did not request an examination, it was standard practice for him to take a patient's vital signs, so they went into the exam room. She was clear with her brittle smile that she wanted to confer with John alone. That was fine with me, it meant she hadn't come to have me chair the next West Adams event.

The next unexpected visitor was Roger, whose senior year in high school did not seem taxing as he often popped into Miss Manley's kitchen for a snack; that afternoon he appeared in the office.

"Hullo. Where are the Crumpets?" he asked. "You know, the Crompton sisters."

"Aren't they in the shed, typing like maniacs to meet a deadline?"

"No. Freya's been sick or something for the last few days. Lying on her stomach and typing in bed, Min said. How odd is that?"

"I'm sure it's nothing serious. You don't seem to have much to do these days."

"They're sick and tired of us. Graduation is in two weeks, which means I won't be able to work at the hotel that day, but I'll rake in the moolah for all my academic achievements."

I had to laugh at his candor. "So, you think all of your family and neighbors will shower you with money?"

"I certainly hope so. That's the way it's supposed to work." He seemed offended that I didn't know that. "Of course, my parents won't be here. I hope they send something exotic from China. And I don't mean a stack of their worthless money."

"Are you expecting a Ming vase?" I asked. "A silk bathrobe?"

"I could hardly swan about Williams College in such a thing. They would think, well, I don't know what they'd think."

He prattled on about his expectations of joining the best fraternity and, due to our proximity to the school and knowing students who attended, he had managed to pick up a surprising amount of information. Which had the best location on campus, not that the campus was large, which had the best food and the best reputation.

"I've always wondered, the best reputation might make you the Big Man on Campus, but is there any other benefit?" He couldn't tell if I was being entirely serious but answered, nonetheless.

"It can certainly get you fixed up with the better-looking girls from other colleges, once they know what house you're in. I don't think the professors care one way or another. But it's supposed to help when you go out into the work world—for instance, if I wanted to work in Hartford or Boston or New York. When you go for an interview and shake hands, you give them the secret handshake and they know you're all right."

Ah, youth, I thought. If it could all be so simple.

"Got to go," he said, breezing out in search of girls or food, his two main preoccupations.

Mrs. Proctor exited the exam room shortly thereafter, and I wondered if he had prescribed some kind of sleeping aid or calming tonic; it had been quite a week for her.

John went to his office, closed the door, and I heard him speaking on the phone. It wasn't a very long call, but he remained there for long enough for me to wonder if there was some problem he hadn't told me about. About ten minutes later, he emerged with a puzzled look on his face.

"What is it?"

"I remember getting a life insurance policy for myself at the recommendation of one of the other doctors. I had inquired about cashing it out last week when the bank loan wasn't available. I thought perhaps they had misunderstood and sent it anyway. But it's not. It's a life insurance payout. For Ellen. We got a policy for her, too. I guess after we divorced, she never changed the beneficiary."

I was speechless. His ex-wife had died not too long ago. She had been so intent on improving her financial situation and all along there had been route to it unforgotten by the women.

"Are there any other appointments this afternoon?" he asked.

"No."

"Let's lock up and take a walk. I need to clear my head."

"Would you like to be by yourself?" I asked.

"No. Keep me company."

I left my cap on the desk, turned the sign on the door from 'open' to 'closed', and followed him across the back gardens to the path that ran behind the houses and led to several trails in the woods.

"Let's walk up to Highfields," he suggested.

It was one of my favorite walks, through the cool shade that slowly climbed toward the big house with its spectacular view of Mount Greylock and a valley below where I had gone blueberry picking with Glenda last year. As we exited the woods there was a grassy area not curated enough to be called a lawn that faced the drive to the mansion. We stopped and admired the house, empty now for many months, the blinds down and the curtains closed.

"I hope you're not thinking of buying it," I said.

"I couldn't afford it anyway. Then we'd have to deal with all those pesky servants. No, I like where I am. But with the money that just came in, we could pay off some of the mortgages on the house and the rest could go either toward buying Doctor Mitchell out or renting an office more on the main drag in Adams."

It wasn't lost on me that he had said 'we.'

He put his arm around me, and I rested my head on his shoulder. Things would work out just fine.

Chapter 18

Nina graciously offered her back garden for Sam and Elsie's wedding reception that Saturday, although Elsie did most of the decorating and baking herself. Sam took off work Friday afternoon to bring over the folding chairs from the church's meeting room and set them up around the same folding tables that had served us well at the Garden Fair. It was going to be a simple ceremony at the church presided by the Reverend Lewis, then back to their house for a cake and punch.

"Haven't they heard of champagne up here?" Minerva asked me as she passed the activity in the backyard.

"How is Freya feeling?" I asked.

"The worst is over. That'll teach her." She laughed. "Or maybe not."

I didn't want to sound like an old fogey, but I wondered if the sisters realized how much gossip centered around them and their carefree attitude toward men. Perhaps they didn't care as they would be back in the larger hunting grounds of New York City at the end of the summer. Miss Ballantine had told me in an arch voice that Mr.

Headley was married, as if it were important to me or that I should somehow slip the information to Freya, but I just raised my eyebrows in mild surprise and said, "How nice."

"Their family owns the paper company in Pittsfield," she said, a fact I already knew.

It always surprised me how prominent men, once they became well known and powerful, could be so careless in their behavior. Was it that they felt above reproach or was it the thrill of being indiscreet and not being caught that propelled them? In any case, I thought Freya's behavior was asking for trouble from the gossipmongers and it could reflect badly on Glenda, who might be assumed to be the chaperone for the Cromptons. Of course, she wasn't, as they were about the same age, but she still might be held accountable for any consequences.

Late Friday, after I had changed into casual clothes, I went to Nina's and asked if she needed any help with the preparations. Although it was to be a simple reception, she and Elsie were in a state of high nervousness about the possible shortfall of plates and glasses, and I volunteered Miss Manley's as a backup. I knew they hadn't invited that many people, but it was still a factor of weddings that the bride should be in a state.

A truck pulled up in the driveway and Mr. and Mrs. Worth, Sam's parents, began to unload armfuls of tree boughs and vines from their farm. Mrs. Worth was a strong, stout woman, cheerful in that stoic New England manner.

Elsie sighed. "Oh, it's going to look beautiful." She began to cry.

"Don't do that or I'll start," Nina said. "It's going to be hard enough to be without you." They hugged each other. "I'm happy that you and your mother-in-law get along so well."

I stepped out into the yard and greeted the Worths, congratulating them on the impending happy event the next day. Turning at a sound behind me, I saw Officer Reed pull into John's driveway although it was after office hours. By the look on his face, he wasn't there to shoot the breeze and I hurried over to see what was happening.

They were already in a deep discussion when I tapped on the door jamb of John's office to announce my presence.

"This is bad," John said.

"Those darned tunnels at Dexter's place. One of them collapsed on him," Officer Reed said.

I put my hand to my mouth in shock. "How do you know?"

"One of the workers called on the telephone Dexter recently installed. They pulled him out from under all the dirt, but he wasn't breathing. I'm taking Doc Taylor up to see if there is anything we can do."

"You'd better stay here," John said to me. "Joanna might need all the emotional support she can get."

"Shall I tell her mother?"

Officer Reed and John glanced at each other. "Perhaps you could tell her there was an accident up at the farm."

I nodded my head at the dreadful task as John took his medical bag, plopped a hat on his head and they quickly left.

My legs were heavy with dread as I went back to Nina's. She could see in an instant that something was very wrong.

"Is Joanna upstairs?" I asked.

"No, she took the baby into town for a walk."

"Thank goodness for that," popped out of my mouth. Not that it would absolve me from telling her about the accident when the time came, but it meant that she hadn't been up at the farm and was safe.

Without saying another word, I walked across the yard, through Miss Manley's garden and into Glenda's back kitchen door. She was seated at the table adjacent to the highchair, cajoling Douglas to eat something from a spoon when all he wanted to do was grab it.

"Hello, Glenda. Is Mrs. Nelson in?"

"No, she took the day off. She'll be back before it gets dark. Do they need some help with the decorations?"

I sat heavily on the other kitchen chair and smiled at Douglas. "Glenda, it's awful. It seems that one of the tunnels collapsed on Farley Dexter."

Her eyes grew wide. "Is he?"

"I think so."

"Poor Joanna. Oh, that's awful. Was she up there when it happened?"

"Nina said she had taken the baby into town for a walk. So, I think not. I hope not."

There didn't seem to be anything else to say, so I went back to Miss Manley's. Annie had finished up in the kitchen and was on her way out to help place the boughs along the back fence before going to the church to string the ivy along the pews. She could tell something was wrong, but I said I was fine and went to give Miss Manley the terrible news. There was nothing left to do but sit and wait until John and Officer Reed got back.

MISS MANLEY COULD OCCUPY herself with knitting as she usually did in the sitting room, but I had no such tactile hobby and fiddled with my wristwatch, got up to look out the French windows, took a turn around the room and sat down again.

"At least look at a magazine," Miss Manley said. "You won't read it, but it will give your hands something to do."

I obeyed and flipped through the pages, certainly not in the mood to read the humor article written by a famous performer and not comprehending any of the words anyway. I slapped the pages shut.

"I'm going for a walk. I won't be gone long," I said. I had to dispel this nervous energy of waiting.

It was early evening but, of course, still light and I walked up the path to Highfields because I knew it was the least populated place to be and I was right. It was the same closed mansion with a melancholy history where one of the former owners had died, and I walked along the driveway past the house to watch the sun fade behind the mountains.

I was overcome with how senseless Dexter's death was, and I was furious that he hadn't done anything about those tunnels until it cost him his life. It was stupid. What was the point of that absurd farm concept in the first place? He might as well have thrown his money in the well. And then, when he finally had something of worth—a wife and child—it was all gone. I felt like screaming to the universe but that wouldn't bring him back. There was nothing to be done but walk a bit further before turning back and facing the scene at home.

Chapter 19

Neither John nor Officer Reed had returned; neither had Joanna or her mother. Shortly after I finished pottering in the dining room and getting the table ready for dinner, the telephone rang. I knew it would be John telling me what happened.

"The poor man. Yes, those cursed tunnels were weakened by either rain or ground shifts and, if he hadn't been wearing that ridiculous cloak, the workmen wouldn't have even known he was down there."

I didn't understand what he was trying to tell me.

"A piece of the cloth was sticking out from the pile of dirt. They said they dug frantically but he was beyond saving. He was already dead. It seems he had been dead for a few hours already."

"Where were they that they didn't see or hear anything?"

"Working in one of the back fields. They couldn't have done anything once the collapse began. He probably suffocated."

What a horrible way to die.

"We're just waiting for the funeral home to get up here to take the body away. Have you been able to talk to Joanna?"

"She's not here. Neither is her mother. I dread having to tell them."

"Yes, awful stuff," John said. "I'll try to be back soon."

I hung up the receiver and leaned against the wall. Dexter had spoken harshly about Mr. King's intentions in condemning the farm. He had been so angry about it that for a moment I had wondered if he might have killed Mr. King. Perhaps he did but I didn't like to think this was some kind of divine retribution. In any case, it was too bad that the Commissioners hadn't acted on the recommendation, or he might still be alive.

I heard the back door open and went into the kitchen to see Glenda with Douglas on her hip.

"What news?" she asked.

I told her what I knew and suggested the revelation to Mrs. Nelson would best come from her employer.

"I couldn't do that. I would hem and haw and go to pieces. Why don't you do it?"

"I'll go with you, but I thought she wasn't home."

"She's not. You don't think she had anything to do with Dexter's death, do you?"

"First of all, it seems to have been an accident. Just because she had an unhappy marriage and has sworn off men doesn't make her a murderer."

Glenda blinked. "You never know. Suppose she is? She's living under my roof and with Stuart gone during the week, I could be in grave danger."

Sometimes her exaggerations were infuriating. "Don't you have a lock on your bedroom door?"

"Yes, but what about Douglas? Look what happened to the Lindbergh baby." She started to cry, and Douglas raised the pitch with his howling.

Miss Manley dashed into the kitchen to ask what the matter was.

"It seems Mrs. Nelson has not returned, and Glenda is upset." I glossed over the more extreme overtones.

"Perhaps she is visiting Joanna next door," Miss Manley suggested mildly although concerned at Glenda's weeping.

"That's a good idea. Let's pop over there to see," I suggested. "Dinner can wait a bit."

Anything to distract my friend who now had child kidnapping on her mind.

Nina was home and we found Reverend Lewis playing with Eleanor on a blanket on the floor. What a charming picture they made, the usually staid minister and the gurgling child.

"I miss Stuart," burst out of Glenda's mouth and a fresh round of crying began. I took Douglas from her and plopped him on the rug next to Eleanor to distract him.

"I worry all the time about something happening to Stuart, and now Dexter's dead and the Nelsons are gone and I'm afraid someone will run off with Douglas. Nina propelled her to the couch and put her arm around her.

"Dexter! What about Dexter?" Nina looked at me.

"I'm afraid he either fell into one of those tunnels on the property or went into one and it collapsed on him."

"How dreadful. Oh, poor Joanna! What's to become of her now."

Glenda raised her head from Nina's shoulder as if to ask what about *her* fears.

"It's not unusual for new mothers to worry about everything, Glenda. Every little sniffle, every too quiet moment, even worrying about what would happen without one's husband," Nina said.

Reverend Lewis looked up with renewed pleasure at knowing what a treasure his wife was before returning to the matter at hand. "The poor man. Joanna can continue to live with us, but where is she? She's been gone a long time and Rosalie must be hungry by now. And she must be told about this."

"We'll take care of it," Nina said. "Why don't you go back home and, if Mrs. Nelson appears, have her come over here."

It seemed cowardly but it was a relief to both Glenda and me not to have to break the dreadful news just yet. I parked her and the baby in Miss Manley's kitchen and gave him a piece of bread to gnaw on until she pulled herself together and admitted it was time for his real supper and went home.

Miss Manley and I had just finished dinner when I heard tapping at the back door and heard John call out my name. I rushed to him, and we embraced.

"Have you had anything to eat?" Why was that almost always the first question?

"No. But not important."

"Come sit in the dining room," Miss Manley said, appearing in the doorway. "We'll get you a plate, and you can update us."

I piled a plate high with the meatloaf and mashed potatoes that Annie had made for us and wondered aloud, "I wish there were something stronger than elderberry wine."

Without a word, Miss Manley disappeared into the pantry and after rooting around behind some cans, produced a glass jar of clear liquid.

"Something someone left behind on a previous visit," she said, meaning the last time Stuart had stayed over. That was some time ago, but mercifully, alcohol doesn't seem to go bad. I got three cordial glasses from the cabinet and poured out the portions. We could all use a drink, I thought.

"Miss Manley, you shouldn't have," John protested, raking his hand through his disheveled hair. "Aggie, you shouldn't have, either, but bless you for that."

We watched him take the first few bites, sitting on the edge of our chairs until he sensed the tension in the room and held up his hand.

"No, go ahead, take your time and eat," I said.

"I'D FEEL BETTER if I told you all about it first. The poor men who found him were beside themselves. They kept saying over and over that Dexter told them never to go near the tunnels because they were dangerous."

"Obviously," I said. "So, what was he doing there?"

"Do you think he had resumed his former mushroom farming and didn't want anyone to know?" Miss Manley asked.

"What an interesting idea," I said. That had never occurred to me.

"I don't think so, although he might have gone down one of the tunnels of his own volition. But I am not convinced it spontaneously collapsed on him."

"Why?" I asked.

"There was too much dirt on him. He was almost encased in soil."

We looked at one another.

"Those flimsy wooden supports that held up the walls weren't broken, either. It looked very suspicious. Naturally, the workmen have been brought into town for additional questioning."

"You don't think they had anything to do with it, do you?"

"The dirt nearby was a mess of footprints, tire tracks and who knows what. Officer Reed parked some distance away, but Dexter's car may have driven over the soft earth as well as some other car, it was hard to tell. Then the workmen had trampled over the entrance as they dug him out with their hands and a shovel they said was nearby."

"Anyone could have left the shovel there," I said. After a few moments, I added, "I suppose this discounts Dexter as the person who killed Mr. King."

"Not necessarily. He may have done so over his anger at being displaced from his farm, but someone else may have had a grudge against Dexter."

My mind whirled with the various comments people had made in the past few weeks. Mrs. Nelson was not pleased with Joanna's choice of him for a husband although I thought it had been better than no visible father at all. But would she jeopardize her daughter's happiness and financial well-being?

We had all observed Mrs. Proctor's prodigious temper both at Mr. King and Dexter, but would she drive up to the farm by herself and be able to take advantage of him and heave him into a tunnel? And then shovel dirt on top of him to make it look like an accident? She was a sturdy woman and a determined one, but that seemed unlikely.

What about Mr. Proctor, the mild-mannered husband? He might have had enough of the antics of the men who had attempted to thwart his wife's ambitions. Nobody would suspect mild-mannered Mr. Proctor, and even I had a hard time imagining him working up the ire to commit such a deed unless he was very good at masking his emotions.

Who else had an interest? Miss Olsen? She was dead set on her mentor getting elected and she had seemed surprised and disappointed that the death of Mr. King did not automatically put her in the assistant's seat as she imagined. She impressed me as more of a follower than a take-charge sort of person—could she have been working with Mrs. Proctor to effect the deaths of both men?

"Aggie?" John asked, disturbing me from my musings.

"I have the sensation you are trying to work this out."

"I am, but none of it makes sense. Yet."

John had barely finished his dinner when Officer Reed came to the kitchen door looking for him.

"There's been a complication," he said, and the two men left with me and Miss Manley wondering what could be worse at this time. I knew Joanna had returned because of the wailing from the Lewises' house when she received the awful news. As we cleaned up in the kitchen, we saw Mrs. Nelson walking briskly across the back gardens from Glenda's house to the Reverend's, so she had been informed as well. All I could think was that the women had experienced such incredible hardships already and now this.

Chapter 20

The telephone rang early the next day before Annie arrived and I was surprised to hear from John.

"I need to cancel the Adams office hours today and help out Gladstone and Reed."

"What's going on?" I asked.

He sighed. "When we found Dexter's body, he was so covered in dirt that I didn't notice that he had been hit on the back of the head. That's what killed him, not suffocation. It seems someone dumped him in that tunnel and then covered him in the dirt to look like an accident."

"Surely someone would know that there would be an examination of the body or an autopsy and it would be revealed."

"That's exactly what happened, but it doesn't get the police any closer to figuring out who was up at the farm or even when the murder took place. The workmen were of no help. They said they hadn't seen Dexter all day."

"What do Gladstone and Reed expect you to do?"

"The funeral director began to clean up the body last night before discovering the wound. Naturally, he stopped and called Gladstone. I'll be participating in an autopsy this morning in Pittsfield. If I'm not back after lunch, I'd like you to go to the office in case anybody comes in."

"Sure," I said.

While John was in Pittsfield, Officer Reed and Inspector Gladstone were back in West Adams, trying to piece together everyone's whereabouts, although the time of death was still not nailed down. From my vantage point behind the dining room curtains, I could see that the two men were bearing down on Glenda's house, ready to give Mrs. Nelson a thorough interrogation.

The distraction allowed Glenda to come over to our place with Douglas to fill us in on what was happening.

"She didn't come back until late yesterday and was very vague about where she had been. They're talking to her now and I don't know if she'll be forthcoming."

"She doesn't have access to a car and the farm is quite a hike—how likely is it that she walked all the way there without being seen?"

"Well, where was she then?" Glenda asked.

"I guess we'll find out soon enough."

We saw the two men tramp across the back gardens to Reverend Lewis's house on the other side of us, presumably to question Joanna. She was the least likely suspect in my eyes, marrying the father of her child, the man who would provide her security and respectability. They were there for under an hour while Glenda, Annie and I speculated about what was going to happen next. Gladstone must have gone out the front way to his car because Officer Reed appeared at our back door by himself.

"Come in, have some tea," Annie said.

He looked exhausted from a long night and an early morning.

"There are some cinnamon rolls if you haven't had anything to eat."

"Bless you," he said.

We stared at him as if he were going to reveal what was going on, but instead he looked uncomfortable, so Glenda hoisted Douglas back up on her hip and went home while I climbed the stairs. The shed behind the Lewises' house came alive with the Crompton sisters carting in piles of paper, likely the latest tome, and they chattered to each other, seemingly unaware of the tragedy that had occurred. Hadn't Glenda told them yet?

I picked up the letter I had written to my parents, where I reassured them that the investigation was ongoing and, of course, my father was above suspicion, not knowing anybody here in West Adams. Being above suspicion may not have been entirely true, but I thought it important to reassure them. I hadn't added anything about Dexter's death and would hold off on telling them for a while; I knew they worried about me and might think I was in danger.

"Off to the post office," I called out to Miss Manley, who was at her desk in the sitting room. Putting my head around the corner I asked her, "Do you need any stamps?" She shook her head and continued writing.

"Thank you, no."

It was a lovely day so far, not too hot for June and a mild breeze swayed the hydrangea blossoms in the front yard. I realized I hardly had time during the week to do any errands and it was pleasant having the morning off. No sooner had I posted my letter with Mr. Bridges than I ran into Mrs. Proctor outside the post office.

"Have you heard?" she asked me in shock, putting her hand on my arm. "How horrible."

My first thought was that she had an extraordinarily strong grip, but I didn't react or say anything and she felt compelled to explain.

"You know I didn't like that young man and I thought his attempts to derail my campaign bordered on the unethical. But I can't help but feel sorry that he died. Mr. King was prescient in wanting to condemn the farm property. From what I hear, it was those dangerous tunnels that finally got to him."

For a moment I wondered how she knew that much so quickly, but I was overlooking the rapid communication system in West Adams. I could be sure that when I got back home, Annie would have the full story to date from Officer Reed and would share it with me.

"I don't know if you were aware, but Mr. Headley and Mr. Campbell have graciously offered to appoint me to fill out the remainder of Mr. King's term. I'm off to Pittsfield shortly to get an overview of the job. What the men won't tell me, my friend Margaret will." It seemed that suddenly everything was working in her favor, and I was annoyed by her smug attitude, as if the deaths of two people didn't amount to much.

"That's nice. Inspector Gladstone is in town here today but I'm sure he'll catch up with you later," I said. She looked surprised at my comment, but I turned on my heel and began my walk home.

A large and expensive car was driving slowly down the street and passed me, then stopped and waited for me to catch up.

"Miss, I'm looking for the Reverend Lewis's home," a well-dressed woman in the back seat called out to me. In the driver's seat was a chauffeur turned out in gray livery with a double row of brass buttons down his chest and a natty cap on his head.

"I'm going that way if you'd like to follow me. It's only a few more blocks."

I glanced back and saw that the license plate was from Connecticut and wondered who it could be. As we approached, I pointed out the house to them, then walked between the properties to Miss Manley's back door.

Annie was alone in the kitchen, immersed in a cookbook that boded well for dinner that evening.

"I'll tell you what I know if you'll share with me," I said, sitting down at the enamel-topped kitchen table.

"What makes you think I know anything you don't?"

I gave her an exasperated look. "Here's what I know: Dexter did not aimlessly trip and fall into one of the infamous tunnels. He was hit on the back of the head, and they only discovered it while cleaning him up. John is participating in the autopsy in Pittsfield even as we speak, and I'll know more when he gets back. And there's a car with Connecticut plates, an expensive car, that has pulled up in front of the Reverend's house."

"I wonder who that could be? Well, Tom Reed didn't tell me anything I didn't already know. But Gladstone is on the trail of Mrs. Proctor, who had everything to gain from killing both Mr. King and Farley Dexter."

"He's going to have a hard time finding her. She's on her way to Pittsfield to get an orientation about her upcoming appointment. Although technically, that appointment won't happen until there is a Board meeting."

"Tom was concerned about that. He said he thinks there is some clause in the State constitution that an elected person can't be arrested for a crime while serving in office."

"What? That's not possible, is it?"

"He said he knew of a State legislator who got in a fistfight with a man and, when the police arrived, he got out of an arrest because the legislature was in session. Maybe that applies to County Commissioners, too."

The doorbell rang and I wondered if it were the woman who sought Reverend Lewis and may have been in error, but it was Mrs. Proctor.

"So sorry to disturb you, but I'm in a bit of a pickle. Miss Olsen was to accompany me to Pittsfield today, but she is under the weather. I hate driving on that winding road by myself—it always makes me nervous. I was wondering if you would come with me?" She smiled sweetly.

Many things went through my mind. I understood her trepidation in encountering the bends in the road and the impatient drivers behind as that had been my reaction, too. But she had lived here most of her life and was surely used to it. Where was Mr. Proctor? Couldn't he have offered to drive her? Or she could have taken the bus as many people did. Why did she assume, correctly, as it turned out, that I wasn't working that morning or that I was free to accompany her? I cocked my head to one side and realized I probably looked like an inquisitive dog and, were I a dog, my ears would have stood up trying to comprehend her motives.

"I saw that you weren't in your uniform...." She smiled again.

A lifetime of being polite and acquiescing to the wishes of my elders extinguished any objections I could manufacture on the spot, so I agreed. I let Annie know the plan and that I would be a back in the afternoon, to which Mrs. Proctor nodded.

Although she had said driving made her nervous, she seemed comfortable enough to me as she took the turns at more than the speed limit. I was the one who was beginning to be nervous as she turned to face me as we talked, and I was silently hoping that she would not talk so much. It didn't work.

"I must confess that I had an ulterior motive in asking you to accompany me today," she began. "I noticed that you have an uncanny ability to size people up and get the lay of the land, so to speak." She turned to look at my reaction.

Keep your eyes on the road, was all I could think.

"I may have mentioned before that something did not sit right with me and the way the County runs its business. I know the elected officials like to point their fingers at the paid administrators, and the staff will blame the Commissioners, although they don't dare to do so for fear of their employment. Even acknowledging that dynamic, what strikes me is that there is general unease in those offices."

"Do you think the staff is afraid?"

"Not exactly. It almost seems as if they are just waiting for someone to ask the right questions, but nobody has," she said. We were getting closer to the car in front of us, so she looked in her side mirror to see if anyone was behind her, stepped on the gas and overtook the sedan easily.

"Slowpoke," she muttered.

I was gripping the armrest while trying to remain calm. Now I understood why Miss Olsen might have felt under the weather if this was the way Mrs. Proctor normally drove.

"Here's my thought: while I am meeting with Mr. Headley and Mr. Campbell, perhaps you could just walk around and take the temperature of the place, if you know what I mean."

I didn't know what she meant. "Talk to people? Ask them questions?"

She pursed her lips. "No, that would be too obvious. Maybe you could pretend that you were interested in past meeting minutes or something. Just to see how people react."

I thought that was a ridiculous idea but didn't say anything.

"Yes, that's it. I do need to see the previous minutes of the meetings and I'll say that I brought you along to collect them. How's that?" That sweet smile again, only this time it seemed it was produced not to cajole me but because she was very pleased with her subterfuge.

"I could do that," I answered. I was thinking she better not ask me to search anyone's desk. Not that I couldn't do it effectively, but she had provided no rationale for it.

She was beginning to slow down as we approached the city, not only because there was more traffic but because there was a prominently displayed speed limit sign. I wondered if Annie's comment about elected officials being immune from the law could be true or if it was one of those legends people liked to relate to one another.

Traffic on North Street was moderate, and she carefully navigated her car to the right-hand lane and turned down East Street.

"There's the building," she said proudly and, as the first woman Commissioner, she had a right to be proud. Despite her ego, her leadership skills would probably be a boon to us all.

We took the elevator up to the top floor and exiting into a lobby with one woman at a desk at the far end.

"Hello, Margaret," Mrs. Proctor said.

The pudgy woman stood and came to shake her friend's hand but remained formal, nonetheless. "Mrs. Proctor, what an honor."

"This is my friend, Miss Burnside, who is here to collect copies of the previous months' meeting minutes."

"Certainly," Margaret said, doing a good job of hiding her surprise. "Please sit down. Can I get you water or coffee?"

"No, thank you. Are the other Commissioners in today?"

"No. I wasn't expecting them. I'm here by myself, it seems."

"I don't want to distract you from your work…," Mrs. Proctor said.

Margaret puckered her brow. "The carbon copies are downstairs, and I'll have to get them. How many months' worth do you think you'll need?"

"At least two years. Also, is there a handbook of protocol or something?"

"Yes. Let me think about where some of those things are. Let me just pop into Mr. Headley's office. He's very tidy and I know exactly where his handbook is." She walked down a short hall, disappeared into an office and came out almost immediately with a large binder. "Found it!"

She handed it to Mrs. Proctor, who was impressed by the size.

"The statutes are in there, quite fine print. I'm sure he won't mind your borrowing it for a few days. We have Mr. King's still, of course, but his office is a bit of a mess. Let me think. I'll see if I can get one of the girls from downstairs to come up here while we go get the other materials."

"Oh, don't bother," Mrs. Proctor said. "I'll stay up here and start my education by reading this." She patted the binder and looked up at me innocently. "Miss Burnside can help you carry back what you need." She opened the binder and exhaled. "Oh, my, this will be daunting."

"We'll be only about ten minutes," Margaret said. "If the telephone rings, the switchboard will know to take a message."

"I'll be just fine." When Margaret turned, Mrs. Proctor looked at me pointedly, tapped her finger on her wristwatch and gave me a look that I took to mean, 'Stall for time.'

Oh, great, what did I get into this time?

Margaret and I rode the elevator down two floors and came out into the County Clerk's offices, according to the gilt lettering on the glass entry doors. There was a desk facing the doors, but no one was there.

"I'm sure Patsy just stepped out for a moment," she said, a bit embarrassed that no one was on duty, and we stood waiting for someone to appear. After a minute or more, Margaret pinged the bell on the desktop. "I hate doing that," she whispered.

A woman put her head around the corner of one of the open doors down the corridor.

"Hello, Margaret. Where's Patsy? What can I do for you?" She came out with a frown at the thought that the secretary to the Commissioners should be kept waiting.

"Oh, Marcia, I need the last two years' meeting minutes."

"We have copies, but they're sorted by month. Would it be all right if I gave you a stack of folders? Sorry, we were going to put together a binder of the minutes for when a new Commissioner is appointed." She looked at me with a question in her eyes.

"I believe that's going to happen sometime soon," Margaret said without elaborating.

"Let's get a cart. It's quite a stack, especially with the various reports and notes from the departments and supporting documents." She went down the hall and around a corner and came back with a wheeled utility cart very much like the ones we used in the hospital. "If you'd like to come with me," she said, propelling it in another direction to a large file room at the opposite end of the floor.

There were at least fifty tall file cabinets and some lateral cabinets, each one labeled.

"Here we are," she said and yanked one open. "Two years? That's a lot of reading. Are you sure you want all that now?" She looked at me.

"Yes, that's what Mrs. Proctor wanted."

The two women were very efficient and fast in taking out the folders and, in a desperate move to buy time, I dropped one that they handed me so the papers spilled onto the floor.

"Oops! I guess that's why I don't work in an office," I said with a lame comment.

"What do you do?" Marcia asked me.

"I'm a nurse."

They tried hard not to laugh, but I started, and it became contagious. "At least I'm not a surgeon," I added to jolly them along.

"How long have you worked here?" I asked Marcia.

"About ten years. I came here right out of high school."

"And you, Margaret?"

"I began in the secretarial pool for the District Attorney. So much paperwork, you know, and a very fast pace. I moved around and worked my way up."

We picked up the last of the papers from the floor, and I fussed with them to make sure they were in the correct sequence.

"You worked with Mr. King for some time?" I asked.

There was a slight hesitation and, as I looked up, there was a reluctance for them to look at each other.

"Of course, since he first won the election." Margaret turned back to the cabinet and reached in for another handful.

"It must be an exciting job," I said.

"To be honest, a lot of time is spent in meetings taking shorthand on the discussions. And then typing up the minutes," Marcia said. "It might be exciting for the Commissioners but it's hard work for us. Especially if there is a contentious subject and the meetings go on for hours."

"I'll bet," I said. I could see that the task was almost done, and I didn't know if I had given Mrs. Proctor enough time to do whatever she was doing. "What's the most interesting and difficult issue you've seen them discuss? Are the Commissioners usually in agreement on their votes, or do they debate? I'm still new to the area, so I haven't attended a meeting yet."

"They have a lot of opportunities to talk to each other—their offices are just across the hall from each other. I've never heard an argument, if that's what you mean," Margaret said.

"No, I meant debate. Are there public debates? I find that fascinating."

"Not really. The issues are pretty cut and dried from their standpoint. It's the constituents who get heated when they make comments."

"Oh, yes, remember that time a farmer insisted that the County roads folks had trespassed on his property?" Marcia asked.

"He insisted that they had knocked down his fence and the cows had got out, one got hit by a car, and he wanted restitution," Margaret added.

"The rules, and you'll see this in Mrs. Proctor's handbook, are that members of the public are limited in how long they can speak. Five minutes. And they are timed. So, this farmer was very clever. He had a large family, and he had his wife and grown children and some neighbors come forward and among the lot of them they used up over an hour." Marcia rolled her eyes at the recollection. "He ended up getting reimbursed for the damages right then and there."

Margaret looked at her wristwatch. "We'd better get going. Poor Mrs. Proctor will be wondering where we've got to."

Poor Mrs. Proctor, indeed.

Chapter 21

I made sure to punch a few of the wrong buttons in the elevator just to stall a bit more, and then as the door to the upper floor was about to open, I faked a loud sneeze to give Mrs. Proctor plenty of warning that we had returned. But as we exited the elevator, she was seated in the same position as before, with the binder in her lap. It appeared she had read through a significant number of pages.

"There you are," she said and then expressed surprise at the amount of paperwork she had requested. "I don't know that I can take all that with me! Perhaps I could leave some of it here and get it later."

It seemed that Margaret was used to the whims of her employers, and being a friend of Mrs. Proctor held no surprises, either, although were I in her shoes, I might have been annoyed at the wasted effort.

"Are you going to be Mrs. Proctor's assistant?" she asked me.

"No, I'm just along for the ride today," I said truthfully. I detected a note of relief in her voice when she sighed.

"I hope it doesn't sound disrespectful, but could I see Mr. King's office?" Mrs. Proctor asked.

"Not at all. It's a bit of a mess, but that's how he liked it. If I asked if he wanted me to tidy up, he would always object by saying he knew where every piece of paper was." She led us down the hall and opened a door to a large room with a window overlooking the buildings below. And she had been right, there were stacks of papers on the floor, on the desk, on the table and even on the chair in the corner of the room. Behind the desk was an old-fashioned wooden wardrobe, and I feared if someone opened it, reams of paper would tumble out.

"Some people like to work like this, I guess," I said, although if I were his constituent, which I suppose I had been, I would have been horrified to see this chaos.

"It's a lovely space," Mrs. Proctor said, walking to the window and looking out, then she turned and picked up a foot-tall bronze statue of what looked like Abraham Lincoln on the desk. She raised her eyebrows, put it down and thanked her friend for letting us in.

We staggered onto the elevator with me carrying a stack of folders and Mrs. Proctor clutching her binder and rode in silence to the ground floor. I was surprised she didn't speak until we piled the paperwork into the trunk and got back in the car.

"Just as I suspected. Those men were up to no good."

"What did you do while I was downstairs trying to keep them distracted?"

"Sorry I put that on you so suddenly, but I saw my chance, and I took it. I didn't bother with Mr. King's office—that's for another time. Mr. Campbell seems to keep next to nothing in his office. It's Mr. Headley's that I can't wait to get into."

"I'm sorry, but I won't be able to help you with that. I was very uncomfortable today and I wouldn't like anyone to think I've been involved in anything shady." I was glad I said it at last.

"Shady! Hah! Once I figure it all out, you'll know who the shady people are."

She pulled out into traffic and drove down the street toward the hospital.

"Look! There's Doctor Taylor," she said, pointing. He was coming down the steps and I asked her to stop and let me out.

"I'll go back with him, if you don't mind," I said.

She smiled at me. "Of course."

I guess our relationship was not such a secret after all. Still, I decided to be decorous since she was still within listening distance. "Doctor Taylor!" I waved and he was surprised. I turned and waved goodbye to Mrs. Proctor, glad to be out of whatever strange business she was up to.

"What are you doing here?" he asked me.

"I'll tell you in the car. How did the autopsy go?"

"I just observed. Two pairs of hands are one too many in such a situation. Poor Dexter. Fractured skull. We're pretty sure it killed him, but whoever hit him in the back of the head wanted to make sure he wouldn't talk and dumped him in the tunnel anyway."

"How can you tell?"

"There was no dirt in his nose and mouth so at least the poor man didn't suffocate."

I shuddered at the thought. "In retrospect, it wasn't very wise when you and I went into those tunnels in April."

"They were crudely made, yes, but the ground was compact enough. Someone tried to make it look like an accident."

"Do you think Mrs. Proctor could have done it?"

He looked at me sharply. "What do you know that I don't that makes you think that?"

As we drove, I told him my suspicions about her and the strange morning in the offices of the County Commissioners.

WE GOT BACK WELL before lunch. John went to his house for a sandwich, and I could smell something cooking on the stove at Miss Manley's as I entered the kitchen. Annie wasn't about, so I lifted the lid on a simmering pot of something with tomatoes and onions and I didn't know what else. I was suddenly very hungry.

Miss Manley was in the sitting room with Annie standing nearby, and they expressed surprise when I walked in.

"You'll never guess! That big car that came to Reverend Lewis's house? That was Farley Dexter's mother," Annie said.

"Oh, no. How awful for her."

"I didn't hear it from Elsie, of course. She's not there anymore. But Mrs. Lewis was bursting to tell someone, and she came over on the pretext of borrowing some sugar. Mrs. Dexter wanted to talk to Joanna by herself. I can't imagine what is going on."

This was distressing. So many things happening at once and the lines of communication between households were severed.

"Are they gone? I mean, Mrs. Dexter. The mother?"

"She drove up from Hartford, was all I got out of it, and she'll be back this weekend."

I was dying to know what that was all about. "Annie, do I need to borrow a cup of sugar from Mrs. Lewis?"

"Yes, good idea!" she said and hurried to the kitchen to get me an empty bowl.

Despite my curiosity, I walked casually to the Lewises' back door, knocked and went in to find Nina in the kitchen with Eleanor in a highchair, propped up with cushions. She was so small that, without them, she might have slid to the floor.

Nina gave me a wide-eyed look and closed the door to the hall. "The most amazing thing has happened. Farley Dexter's mother came to our house."

"Yes, yes, I know. And?"

"And she wanted to meet Joanna and the baby and she was very polite and civil. And she informed Joanna that as his widow, she inherited his trust fund."

"That was kind of her to come up to tell her that."

"And it is a substantial amount. He may have looked like a vagabond, but he was very well off. Mrs. Dexter suggested she and the baby come live in the house in Hartford. Just think. She and her mother were paupers not so long ago and now she has a steady income and, once she sells the farm, even more to live on. It's like a fairy tale."

"I'd better pretend to take that cup of sugar," I said. "Annie has made something wonderful for lunch and the payback is the information I'll give her."

I slipped out the back and thought about the turnaround in Joanna's fortunes. Who could have imagined? But then my logical, if not suspicious, mind thought about how this came to be. Mrs. Nelson was the one who brought her daughter up to West Adams to work at the farm although she was already pregnant. Did Mrs. Nelson suspect Farley was the father? If so, surely she wouldn't have wanted to kill off her son-in-law, even if she didn't approve of him. Except she must have suspected already that he was wealthy. Joanna was such an innocent. Or was she? Once married, did she collude with her mother to do away with Dexter? Joanna could go live in Hartford in what must be a wealthy home, or she could stay up here and live at the farm with her mother. Could she go back to the farm after what happened there? I was starting to look at the Nelsons in a different, disturbing light.

Chapter 22

The strangest thing was that while I had suspicions about the motivations of the Nelsons, Inspector Gladstone seemed to home in on me. As usual. He called me at the West Adams office and asked me to come to the police station there for an interview.

I looked at John in shock. "What could he possibly think I have done?"

"Not what you have done, but what you may have seen or known, I expect."

"John, I don't trust that man at all. First, he tried to pin the attack on Mr. King on my father—and I'm not so sure he doesn't still believe it. Then, lo and behold, who is Mr. Burnside's daughter but the snooping Nurse Burnside." I was getting quite worked up by my description.

John pulled me into an embrace. "Snooping is much too harsh. Inquisitive, I would say."

I looked up at him crossly. "Thanks a lot."

"Being curious is a talent, a healthy aspect of a person's intellect. Don't be ashamed of it."

I took a compact out of my handbag and checked that my hair was in place. I gave myself one more good look and thought that I looked like a very respectable person, not guilty of anything at all. Unless you were to consider the subterfuge with Mrs. Proctor that morning, the details of which I had only partially shared with John.

I considered changing my clothes before heading to the police station and then reconsidered. My nurse's uniform was a confirmation of my serious intentions and it tended to intimidate some people. Good. As if Gladstone would be intimidated by me.

The surprise I got when I entered the police station was seeing Mrs. Proctor seated in the reception room, looking both defiant and a bit frightened. I smiled at her and sat beside her while Gladys, the secretary, got Officer Reed, who looked glum at having to interview me. But I was wrong, he brought both of us into a room at the same time. That was unusual until I thought that the devious Gladstone hoped to get us to somehow contradict each other, or 'break us' as the police procedural novels said.

Inspector Gladstone was unctuous in his formal greeting to us, and I could sense that Officer Reed wished he were elsewhere.

"Sit down, sit down, I just have a few questions for you fine ladies."

I was stone-faced but I noticed that Mrs. Proctor, normally in full command of herself, was clutching her handbag.

"Now," he began, flipping through that infernal little notebook of his, "let's go back to the events of the Garden Fair."

"Oh, really, Inspector, you can't imagine that a recitation of the events of that day, minute by minute, blow by blow, are going to help you at this point?" I asked.

He was not pleased by my question and tried to stare me down with his beady eyes.

"Well, then," I said, attempting to comply. "What would you like to know exactly?"

"How well do you know Mrs. Proctor, here?"

She and I looked at each other, puzzled.

"As well as I know any of the ladies in West Adams. She participates in Miss Manley's tea group, and she organized the Garden Fair." I wondered why he was wasting our time with this.

"And she is also a patient of Doctor Taylor?"

I looked at her to allow her to answer as I thought it was a breach of confidentiality for me to affirm or deny that fact.

"Yes," Mrs. Proctor answered. "He's the doctor in town." She scoffed and he, instead of being annoyed by her reaction, smirked.

"Isn't it true that you visited him not too long ago?"

"Yes."

"And wasn't the nature of your complaint what is commonly referred to as 'women's problems?'"

She glared at him and then at me.

I flushed, thinking that she assumed John and I had discussed the reason for her visit, which we hadn't.

"And that he prescribed something because of your flashes and outbursts of anger."

"I should say not!" she said angrily, immediately realizing the trap he had set for her.

"Just to set the record straight, on the occasion when Mrs. Proctor came in, she met with the doctor alone. He did not discuss the reason for the appointment, and he is not in the habit of talking about private conversations with patients." I didn't know how viable an excuse that was, but I valued my reputation and had to say it.

She nodded at me, somewhat mollified.

Ignoring my comment, Gladstone went on. "Isn't it true that you have been subject to, shall we say, violent outbursts from time to time? I've heard you described by several people as someone who doesn't suffer fools kindly."

"I would agree that's a fair assessment," she said, lifting her chin proudly.

He flipped through the pages of the notebook. "And you had words with the postmaster, Mr. Bridges, recently."

"What?"

"You were overheard calling him an overpaid bureaucrat." He looked up.

She colored slightly and he knew he had hit the mark.

"And then, let's see…." He turned more pages. "Here it is. An angry and vocal speech made at a County Commissioners' meeting where you stated that they were not concerned with fixing a certain bridge nearby."

"That's entirely true. No one in West Adams would disagree with that statement."

"Except you also said that the three men were acting like a bunch of hooligans."

Now her dander was up. "I certainly did say that. Again, very few people in this town would disagree."

"But most importantly, on the day of the Garden Fair, you made a point to dress down Mr. King about 'electioneering.'"

"And again, I admit having said that. Inspector Gladstone," she began haughtily, "We may seem like an insignificant small town to you. And indeed, we are small in size, but large in sentiment for our community. Our Christmas Tree lighting in December is highly praised. But the Garden Fair is the most important fundraising event and, as you may have heard, drew people from all over the county. We raise money for the repairs of the church building, a prominent structure in our little town. I was not pleased that the County Commissioners took the opportunity to boast about their accomplishments—which are minuscule—and make vapid promises concerning their future endeavors. It was inappropriate, and I felt it my obligation as the Chair of the Garden Fair Committee to say something. And," she added more forcefully, "there were several people who came up to me afterward and commended my comments."

If she thought she had dressed him down, she didn't know Inspector Gladstone as I did.

"There came a time toward the end of the Fair when you yelled something at him, pointing your finger."

"Yes, I did. If you know your world history, there is a famous incident called the Dreyfus affair in France where an officer was wrongly accused of treason. He was defended publicly by the great Emile Zola, who used the expression, 'J'accuse' in a newspaper article."

Gladstone crinkled his face in confusion. "What has that got to do with a bridge in Berkshire County."

"It has to do with ineptitude, something you may be familiar with."

Oops. She went too far on that one and Gladstone glared at her.

"I will be working to remedy the bridge situation after I'm sworn in as County Commissioner next week." Her chin went up in triumph. "And the first thing I may do is make sure that you are no longer working in your position."

"Is that so? Well, let me tell you, Mrs. Proctor, that I do not work at the behest of the County Commissioners. I work for the Sheriff of Berkshire County. And he is an elected official, as you one day may be." He snapped his notebook shut.

They continued to glare at one another until he broke the contest by looking in my direction.

"But, back to Nurse Burnside, here." That awful smile. I could hear Officer Reed shift in the creaky wooden chair behind us.

"You assisted Mrs. Proctor in organizing the Garden Fair, is that correct?"

"Yes."

"And you participated in a campaign committee meeting?"

I looked toward her, wondering if she had supplied this information during a previous interview with him.

"Yes, at her invitation."

"And why was that?"

I stammered a moment. "She said because I had lived in New York City, she thought I had some expertise in politics."

"Is that true?"

"Sadly, no. I wasn't able to add much to the discussion."

"But you are connected to the legal profession, are you not?"

I blinked. "You know my father is an attorney, if that's what you mean."

"That precisely what I mean. Were you aware that your father agreed to represent Mrs. Proctor in legal matters?"

My head swung in her direction, but she did not meet my eyes. "No, I had no idea."

"Is he a criminal defense attorney?"

"No, not at all."

"Don't you think it's strange that Mrs. Proctor didn't tell you about the connection?"

"No, there is something called attorney-client confidentiality. He wouldn't have told me, and Mrs. Proctor didn't have any obligation to share that information."

Where was he going with this?

"This is what I find peculiar. Mrs. Proctor has a vendetta against Mr. King and the other Commissioners, but particularly Mr. King. She chews him out at a public meeting, scolds him again at the beginning of the Garden Fair and then lets him have it at the end of the event. Your father witnesses those exchanges as well as some insinuating remarks that Mr. King made toward you. You have been a strong supporter of Mrs. Proctor in her altruistic affairs and now her political career." He held his hand up to stop me from interrupting. "You accompanied her to Pittsfield to collect some background papers or something. Your father, an attorney, was engaged by Mrs. Proctor the day of the Garden Fair. Mr. King was killed the day of the Garden Fair. The murder weapon was your father's cane. Are you beginning to see a connection?"

There was a cold feeling in my stomach as I realized this horrible man was trying to accuse the three of us—Mrs. Proctor, my father and me—of conspiring to murder Mr. King.

Chapter 23

I managed to stand up and said, "I have nothing further to say to you, Inspector Gladstone." And with my dignity mostly intact, I turned on my heel and left.

"Indeed!" I heard Mrs. Proctor pronounce as she followed me out of the interview room.

We walked silently to the street, and I turned left to go back to Miss Manley's. Mrs. Proctor grabbed my arm.

"I'm sorry, I probably should have told you about talking to your father. But it isn't as the inspector imagines."

"That information would have been helpful. I guess you can see how this looks now." I glanced at my watch. "I have to get back to work," and I strode away, furious with her and annoyed that my father had taken her on as a client. Did he agree before or after Mr. King was found dead? My mind was whirling with unpleasant thoughts, and I stopped by Miss Manley's instead of going directly to the office.

She wasn't at home, and I would tell her later that I had to make a long-distance call. I took a deep breath and called my father's office, something I had done only on rare occasions.

His secretary answered and put me through.

"Agnes, what a surprise! Is everything all right?"

"No, nothing is right." I felt my throat tighten and I was worried that I would start to cry, but I needed to maintain my composure. "I have just been interviewed by Inspector Gladstone. He said that Mrs. Proctor had hired you to be her lawyer."

"No, that's not correct. She asked me to refer her to somebody for estate planning purposes."

"Oh. But you're in New York and we're in Massachusetts. Why did she ask you?"

"I thought that was odd, but I agreed to call around and refer her to someone in your state. Perhaps in her public position, she didn't want to consult somebody local. I have some feelers out and will get back with her soon enough."

"Inspector Gladstone was implying that she and you and I were somehow connected to Mr. King's death."

"That's ridiculous. I think Gladstone was just stirring the pot, trying to get you to say something that you shouldn't. After all, you've got nothing to hide." He paused. "Do you?"

"Of course not!" Unless he meant my assistance as an accomplice in her examination of the Commissioners' offices. "I'm glad I asked you, though. I feel better about it."

"That's good, dear." We had a few moments of family chat after that, and I let him get back to work.

While I was reassured that I could not be implicated in a murder conspiracy, I was furious with Inspector Gladstone's insinuations. He had already interviewed my father and, if he couldn't see that he was a rational person, then he was as inept as Mrs. Proctor had declared him. It was too bad she couldn't fire the man. He had done nothing but muddy the waters and get people needlessly agitated.

John could see that I was upset when I reappeared at the office.

"The famous Gladstone touch at work again?" he asked.

"That man is awful! He had Mrs. Proctor in the same room with me as if we were in on Mr. King's death together and one of us would rat the other out, as they say."

"I hope you did use the term 'rat' to him," John said, smiling and trying to lessen the tension.

"No, I didn't. I didn't use any of the terminologies from those gangster movies you like so much."

"You mean like, 'Take that, copper!'" He began to laugh and, released from the strain of the day, I laughed at his James Cagney impersonation.

"Do you know she threatened to fire him?" I asked.

"Mrs. Proctor is getting to be a force with which to be reckoned already!"

"He also suggested that she had come to see you about 'the change' as if the menopause were causing her to act irrationally."

"Who could have told him that? The reality is that she had noticed some changes in her husband's behavior and wondered if she should bring him in for a checkup."

"That's reassuring," I said. But as the afternoon wore on and patients came and went, I began to think that perhaps Mr. Proctor might have decided to take matters into his own hands when it came to people who stood in the way of his wife's honor and ambitions.

We were just finishing up about five-thirty when Glenda stopped by and expressed surprise that I was still at work. John came out of his office, expecting another drop-in patient, and was pleased that it was just a social call.

"Doctor Taylor, I think you have been working Aggie all too hard lately."

He and I were both surprised at her comment.

"The advice of my pediatrician in New York is that I need to get out more and be with actual adults from time to time instead of just the baby."

"That sounds like good advice," John agreed.

"It was more like a prescription. And in that event, considering that my mental and physical health are at risk, I have come to ask that Aggie have tomorrow afternoon off to accompany me to Pittsfield."

"To see a doctor?" I asked.

"No, silly. To go shopping. And maybe have dinner. What do you say?"

"I say yes," I said, perhaps too quickly.

"Let's look at the appointment book," John said, affecting a stern face. He turned the pages slowly just to get Glenda to exhale with impatience. "I suppose I can spare her tomorrow afternoon."

She clapped her hands like a child. "That's wonderful. I've been dragging along in these old clothes for months and I need something new. This will be so much fun!" She turned to go.

"Thank you, Doctor," and charmed him with her smile.

We both laughed at her exit, and I thanked John for his understanding.

WHAT FUN it was to be in the passenger seat with Glenda behind the wheel, the windows down and our hair blowing about, the scent of mown grass as we passed one stretch of lawn.

"We have to do this more often," she said, above the road noise.

"I think you should get your New York doctor to write an actual prescription—you know, on his pad—and then it would seem entirely legitimate," I said.

"That's a spectacular idea. I want to take full advantage of Mrs. Nelson's being around. Since she found out about Joanna's good fortune, she might decide to move in with her in Hartford."

"Has Joanna said she was going to do that? What about the farm?"

"That darned farm! It has been nothing but trouble. She'd be better off selling it and keeping the money to buy a habitable house."

"Who would want to buy the place in the condition it's in?"

That was the question. There were still all the tunnels that hadn't been filled in, and I didn't know if the mushroom-growing enterprise had continued in secret. The house needed a huge number of essential improvements, such as central heating and better sanitary accommodations. What about the workers? Were they owed anything? And once they were paid off, where did they have to go? I let my mind wander down that path until we had to slow down for a mowing machine that was trying to tame the wild growth on the side of the road. Rampant growth in the summer would be a barren shoulder on the roadway just a few months away.

"Where shall we go first? I'm dying to get new shoes. I've been wearing these forever and I'm sick of them."

"I know you're anxious for a change, but why not wait until you go back to the City next month?"

"Don't be ridiculous, Aggie. The selection in New York is mind-boggling but the prices are so much higher. We'll get a total deal here."

"Do you think we'll have time to stop by the library?"

She looked at me in astonishment. "Your first afternoon off and you want to read books?"

"No, I want to check some out. Let's go to England Brothers, then stop by the library, which will still be open, and then we'll have dinner. Sound good?"

"It sounds perfect," she said.

We parked on North Street in front of the imposing building, and I could hear Glenda sigh in anticipation.

"Do you have a budget or are we just going to go crazy inside?" I asked half in jest.

"I have been a frugal housewife up here and stashed some money away. I wonder if my mother's old charge account is still available?" she asked aloud as we got out of the car. "Wouldn't that be amazing? Let's go upstairs to the billing department and I'll find out."

Probably the last thing that Stuart wanted to find out was that Glenda could charge to her mother's now re-activated account. The saleswoman expressed her sympathy at Mrs. Butler's death the previous year and commented on how prompt she had always been in paying her bill. I wondered if that was true or a mild hint to all potential buyers to do the same. A new card was typed up with the old account number and we were off and running. We had about two and a half hours to shop and we hadn't even got off the billing floor when Glenda saw the children's department and began to ooh and ahh at the charming clothes on display.

"Just look at this sailor suit. Douglas would look so cute in it. Have you seen the little girls' dresses?"

"Yes, Glenda, but let's keep on task or we'll never get to buy you anything."

"Sometimes I wish I had a baby girl," she said wistfully.

"Next time," I patted her arm.

She bought the sailor suit, and a light blue cotton sweater and was tempted to get him shoes but I talked her out of the idea with the sound reasoning that she should get them when he learned to walk, as opposed to now when he was just trying to crawl. Who knows how much his feet might grow by then?

I could see the delight in her eyes, holding the card out to each saleswoman as the purchases were rung up. No need to send the money in a pneumatic tube to accounting. Just scribble the account number on the receipt and on to the next department.

Lest you think Stuart and his reactions to this buying spree were not on her mind, Glenda was careful to select a tattersall shirt and a sporty tie for her husband after perusing a stack of other selections.

"There. Now he can't say I was being selfish. On to the women's department!"

Our arms were full of packages since she had me carry some and we plopped them in a chair while looking through the well-spaced racks of dresses.

"This is darling!" was said more than once and the astute saleswoman, seeing the packages and hearing a dedicated shopper in her midst, was more than happy to assist. Another chair was available for me to sit in while Glenda tried on each dress, vowing to only get two at the most, but the selection was too tempting. She narrowed it down to three and chewed a finger while she decided.

"Price or nice?" she asked me.

"All three are nice. Is the price differential that great?"

"Here's what I'll do. I'll get all three and when Stuart comes up next weekend, I'll ask him which ones I should keep. I can return them if I haven't worn them, isn't that right?" she asked the woman.

"Of course," she answered, knowing she'd get her commission upfront and the likelihood of return was slim. She took the dresses on their hangers, holding them out like some ritual offering, off to the backroom to package them up.

I looked at my wristwatch. "Do you think you can get a pair of shoes in forty-five minutes?"

"I hope so. Otherwise, we'll have to come back on Saturday."

"No, Glenda, I need to have my weekend." I propelled her to the stairs, now loaded down with packages and the dresses. "If you give me your car keys, I'll put these in the trunk."

"Great idea. No use being weighed down."

My chore done, I found her seated in front of several boxes of shoes while a saleslady gushed about the lovely low-heeled, T-strap shoes made of light tan leather. They were beautiful and when Glenda walked around like a mannequin, you could see that they elongated her legs in a flattering way.

"So, we're done?" I asked, half-seriously.

"Aggie, any other girl would be tearing through the boxes looking for the perfect pair of shoes."

"I've got my nurses' whites to wear most days and casual flats for the rest of the time. I'd love a pair like that but have very few places to wear them."

"Let's see if they have a pair in your size." She sent the saleswoman off to fetch them.

"I appreciate the thought, but the idea of us showing up back in West Adams in matching shoes is too silly."

"Only if we go back and get you a matching dress."

I tried them on anyway and they were becoming, but I stopped myself from getting attached because I wanted to save my money for something bigger in the future. I wasn't sure what yet, but after all, Madame Celestina had predicted a change coming my way.

Glenda bought the shoes. We continued browsing until we heard the bing-bong tone letting us know that the store would be closing soon.

That was one disadvantage of shopping here rather than in the City, where the stores stayed open later.

We exited to a still bright late afternoon and drove to the library. They had a special shelf where the newest best sellers were located, and you usually had to put your name on a list to get one. I felt my life was serious enough that I could indulge in the absurd books of E. F. Benson, especially **Lucia in London**. I can't remember how I became interested in the series, which was light as a feather and funny, but that volume wasn't available. Looking on the regular shelves, **Mapp and Lucia** was there, and I grabbed it.

I went to find Glenda, who was leafing through a fashion magazine, and she frowned at my choice of volume. "Maps? What do you want with that?"

"I'll tell you later."

I checked out the book, glad that I had had the foresight to get a library card on one of my previous visits to the city, and we decided to have an early dinner. There was a restaurant with a Robin Hood theme; why, I'm not sure, but it was refreshing to be off our feet and about to indulge in someone else's cooking.

"Mrs. Nelson is getting quite a bit better. I think the Crompton sisters gave her a few pointers. They were hardly starving, but I think they were going hungry having to face some of the menus she concocted."

"It's probably coming from that impoverished setting that drove her to make filling, if not delicious, meals."

We ordered steak, a great treat, and baked potato. But first, the waiter brought us each a wedge of iceberg lettuce with a bleu cheese dressing dribbled over the angle of the leaves. It was refreshing and tangy and, although Annie was a fantastic cook, one of the most exotic things I had eaten in a long time.

We lingered over coffee after dinner while Glenda grumbled about not being able to have a cocktail before deciding it was time to drive home. The sky was still light although the sun had dipped behind the mountains, and we went slowly along North Street looking at the closed shops. As we approached the perpendicular East Street, I saw Mr. Proctor standing on the corner, looking in all directions.

"I wonder what he's doing here?" I asked.

Glenda slowed down as there was light traffic, and we caught his eye. He motioned us to pull over and came quickly to the car.

"Have you seen my wife?"

"No," Glenda said. "We've just finished dinner."

"She was supposed to meet me here on the corner about a half hour ago."

I thought it odd that she instructed her husband to meet her at a usually busy intersection but said nothing.

"Where has she been?"

"She said she was doing some research." He pushed his hat back on his head and rubbed his eyes in frustration.

I thought about Mrs. Proctor's conversation with John about her husband's behavior. Could it be that he had come to Pittsfield by himself and somehow imagined that she had been with him? If he drove her here, why wasn't he with her while she did the research?

"Did she go to the library?" I asked.

"No, she went to the County buildings. But they're locked up. Where could she have gone?"

"Perhaps you should go to the police station and report it," I suggested.

He looked greatly relieved. "Of course, maybe she forgot that she was supposed to meet me here and thinks I am the one who is lost." He laughed. "Thank you." He turned and took a few steps down North Street before coming back. "I forgot where I parked my car."

And looking around, he suddenly said, "There it is." He went to his car and drove toward the police station.

Glenda looked at me. "Is he all there?"

"I don't know, but I wonder if Mrs. Proctor inadvertently got locked in the County buildings."

"Let's go see," Glenda said, and she maneuvered the car onto East Street and parked in front of the building. We walked up the steps, pulled on the locked doors and peered through the glass, but the lights were off in the corridor and no watchman was in view. We knocked on the doors but, seeing no one inside, thought Mr. Proctor must have been mistaken.

We started slowly down the steps and heard a voice behind us. "Ladies? Can I help you?"

It was Mr. Headley, hat in hand with the door ajar.

We scrambled back up the steps and told him the tale of the missing Mrs. Proctor.

"That's odd," he said, giving us his dazzling smile. "You can't be locked in. You can open it from the inside and after hours, it locks behind you. See." He let the door close and demonstrated by rattling the handle that it was indeed locked. "Do you think Mr. Proctor might be mistaken?"

"I guess so," Glenda said. "Thank you anyway." We walked back to the car and drove away down East Street.

"Something about that man…," I began, not likely the easy manner in which Mr. Headley had deflected our interest.

"What?"

"Drive around the block, let's see where he goes."

Glenda did so and as we turned off North Street for the second time that night. We saw him take keys out of his pocket and reenter the building.

"Stop the car!" I said in a loud whisper although there was no chance he could hear us.

"Can you pull into the alley? There must be some other way into the building."

"Aggie, what are you talking about?"

"Isn't it obvious? Mrs. Proctor was looking for something in that building. That's what she meant by research. Either she found it and he found her, or I stupidly just let him know that she might be in the building."

Glenda gaped at me.

"Come on," I said, getting out of the car, closing the door quietly and walking up the alley looking for another door into the building. There were wide double doors at the back at the top of a dock for deliveries but those opened only from the inside. There was a single door around the corner, but it was locked when I jiggled the handle.

Then I looked up. A fire escape.

Glenda had followed my glance and she had one word. "No."

"Come on, it's entirely sturdy."

"I'm afraid of heights."

"Don't look down, that's the key."

"Oh, Aggie...," she said in a pitiful voice.

I had to reach up to pull down the initial set of iron stairs and put my foot on the bottom rung. It rocked a bit, which was not reassuring, but these things were meant to carry burly firemen and policemen. They would surely support the two of us.

I climbed up to the second tier and looked back to see Glenda's terrified eyes focused on her hands as she mounted very carefully and slowly. I couldn't wait for her and, when I got to a second-story window, I pushed on the exterior sill which didn't budge. I pushed on the jamb on both sides a little with the palm of my hand in case it was just stuck, but that made the fire escape sway and Glenda gasped.

"Shh!" I said.

"Don't ever do that again!" she said quietly.

Up another story and another stuck or locked window.

"Are you going all the way to the roof?"

"That's a good idea."

"No."

"Then wait there and I'll come back and get you."

"No!" She scrambled to catch up to me.

The fifth floor turned out to be the lucky one and, because the window was already open about six inches, I was able to push it fully upward and climb onto the top of the radiator. I reached my hand out to Glenda, who finally had the nerve to look down, and I thought she would faint.

"Come on," I said, making her sit on the sill before swinging her legs into the room.

"I'll hate you forever for this," she said. "And look at my skirt! Don't they ever dust things in here?"

"We have to be quiet. Mr. Headley is still in the building and I'm betting Mrs. Proctor is here, too. If she is looking for evidence—she'll be on the top floor." I opened the door carefully and looked down the hall in both directions. Glenda followed me as we walked quietly. I had to grab her hand as she was about to push the elevator button.

"What?" she whispered.

"Let's not announce to the entire building that someone is here using the elevator."

We made our way to the stairwell and started climbing, with Glenda muttering behind me with every step. In no time we had got to the Commissioners' floor. I looked through the glass window in the door to see if anyone was about, but it was dark and quiet.

"We have to be incredibly quiet," I said.

"Can I stay here?"

I gave her a withering look and opened the heavy door. We tiptoed into the central reception area, stopped and listened for any sounds. The doors to Mr. King's and Mr. Headley's offices were closed but Mr. Campbell's was open. I motioned for Glenda to follow me and looked around the open door. Nobody there.

Next, I tiptoed to Mr. King's office and slowly opened the door. The window blinds were down and, from what I could see in the gloom, it was much as I had seen it before, with stacks of papers, books and files all over.

I was about to close it when I heard the deliberate tapping of a typewriter down the hall. I grabbed Glenda's hand and yanked her in behind me.

"That came from Mr. Headley's office," I whispered.

"We already knew he was in the building. But what is he doing? He has a secretary to do his correspondence." She gasped and pointed to the corner. There sat Mrs. Proctor, tied up in a chair, a gag around her mouth, her eyes as large as saucers, silently pleading for help.

Chapter 24

I put my finger to my lips and whispered, "Don't worry, we'll get you out of here. Let me just take off this gag. But don't talk. Glenda, stand near the door and listen for Mr. Headley."

I had no sooner loosened the gag than Mrs. Proctor gasped and whispered. "He's going to kill me. He caught me looking in his office. Quick, get me out of this." She squirmed as if that would loosen the bonds.

"Psst!" Glenda called and raced over to me. "The typing has stopped. I think he's coming."

"Sorry," I said to Mrs. Proctor as I refastened the gag, but more loosely this time. Mr. King's office had a wooden wardrobe behind the desk, and I hoped when I opened it, that it wouldn't be full of papers. It wasn't, just an overcoat and an umbrella and I pushed Glenda into it and stuffed myself in as well.

We waited and listened and heard nothing.

"Are you sure you heard the typing stop?"

"Yes."

We waited no more than a few minutes—which felt like an hour—and then heard the doorknob turn. Why hadn't I thought to lock the door?

"There you are," Mr. Headley's smooth voice said to Mrs. Proctor. "I've just finished typing your suicide note."

Glenda put her hand over her mouth.

"You know, you were so angry with Mr. King that you just couldn't help but silence him. But now, after working in his office even for these few days, you realized what a terrible thing you had done, and you just couldn't live with yourself."

I could hear her grunting in protest.

"Let's keep the gag on a bit longer, all right? I don't think I could stand to hear your voice ever again. It will be the last thing to come off before you leap to your death from the roof."

Mrs. Proctor was screaming but it was a muffled noise.

"Let's see. We'll put it on the desk where your dear friend Margaret will find it in the morning. Oh, she will be sad."

I heard papers rustling on the desk in front of us.

"There. Now, let's get the bindings off your feet at least so you can walk up to the roof with me."

Through the crack in the wardrobe doors, I could see Mr. Headley bend down. I smashed open the door of the wardrobe as hard as I could, which sent him crashing to the floor. I don't think he knew what hit him, and then when he did, I attacked him with the umbrella, not the sturdiest of weapons. He shielded his head until he realized it was a young woman who attacked him, and he grabbed my legs and we tumbled to the ground.

Glenda was screaming by then and she was kicking him in the back, which didn't do me much good. He put his hands around my throat and, although I had my right leg bent between us, his arms were long and were increasing the pressure, a horrible grimace on his face. He was very strong, and I could tell I was about to lose consciousness.

Then there was a crash. He fell to the side, knocked out by the bronze Abraham Lincoln statue Glenda had smashed into his head.

I gasped and grabbed my own throat in reflex, then quickly got up.

Glenda and I took the gag out of Mrs. Proctor's mouth and undid the bindings, which shortly were around Mr. Headley's feet and hands, connected in the back for good measure.

"Is he dead?" Glenda asked.

I felt for a pulse. "No."

"That's a good thing. He'll have a lot of explaining to do about how he has misused the taxpayers' money. Along with his pal, Mr. King."

"What about Mr. Campbell?" I asked, my voice hoarse.

"That remains to be seen. Hadn't we better call the police?" She had made a fast recovery and was taking charge already.

I picked up the telephone and noticed my hand was shaking so I handed the receiver to Glenda. "I don't know the number," she said.

"I know Gladstone's number. He'll be thrilled to know we solved another case for him."

It was less than ten minutes after making the call that we heard a siren coming down the street. We had taken the elevator down to the first floor to let him in and saw Gladstone, Mr. Proctor and another police officer racing up the steps. Mr. and Mrs. Proctor embraced and for the first time she broke down in sobs.

"He was going to kill me! He wanted to make it look like I killed Mr. King. He's been working to discredit me all along, telling lies in the community." Mr. Proctor's eyes were filled with tears as he patted her on the back.

"Where is he?"

"Trussed up in Mr. King's office," Glenda said proudly. "Aggie can't speak too well as he was trying to throttle her to death."

Gladstone's eyes widened and he looked at my neck, which was certainly red and likely to be black and blue in no time.

I nodded and felt tears begin to prick my eyes, too, at the near miss.

"I bopped him over the head with Mr. King's statue of Abraham Lincoln. Poetic license or something," Glenda said.

The Proctors sat down on a bench in the entryway while the rest of us took the elevator back up to the Commissioners' floor. This time, I turned on the light in Mr. King's office and observed the mess, with the inert body of Mr. Headley behind the desk.

"You put up quite a fight!" Gladstone said with admiration. With all the papers strewn about and the chairs knocked over, it looked like a barroom brawl had happened. He wasn't aware that, except for the displaced furniture, it hadn't looked much different before.

To save my voice, I pointed to the typed note that Mr. Headley had left on the desk. Gladstone didn't touch it but read it over and shook his head.

"This is bad, very bad."

"I'll say," Glenda piped up.

"It will look bad for everyone in the county, and trust in public officials will be entirely eroded." He looked at the other officer.

I looked at them both sternly and croaked, "I didn't almost lose my life for a cover-up. He was an evil man, as was Mr. King. Mrs. Proctor has the evidence. The citizens will elect a new slate in November."

Gladstone nodded. "There is a mechanism to appoint honest people in their place until then. Let's call an ambulance and get this excuse of a human out of here."

Chapter 25

Glenda was so worked up by this time, worrying about Douglas, who was in capable hands, asking me if I thought she would be arrested for assaulting Mr. Headley, which I thought was unlikely considering that he was trying to choke the life out of me when she knocked him out, until finally she realized that she was one of the heroines of the evening. This last thought was profound since she still had reservations about not finishing up her nursing degree and becoming a mother so early in her marriage. She was almost incandescent with the knowledge that she had participated in something monumental.

We were some hours at the police station in Pittsfield while statements were taken, this time in separate rooms, so I didn't get the full story of what Mrs. Proctor found out or the linkage between the Commissioners. While I had no feelings for Commissioner Campbell one way or the other, I hoped he hadn't been drawn into the schemes of the other two. Even if he hadn't, there was a good chance that the citizens of Berkshire County wouldn't reelect him.

For once, I was not being interrogated by Inspector Gladstone but by one of the city's police officers, an affable young man who could see that speaking was still painful and tried to pose questions that could be answered by yes or no. It was still a tedious procedure and quite late when he said I was done.

To my surprise, John was waiting for me in the reception area, and we shared a long and warm embrace.

"How are you?" He tilted my head back slightly to look at my neck. "That bastard."

"It's all over." I felt tears welling up in my eyes.

"Please tell Mrs. Glenda Manley that I am taking Aggie home," he said to the young officer who had escorted me out.

The world felt different as we drove back to West Adams in silence with John looking over at me from time to time.

Finally, he said, "Let's get you some pain medication so you can sleep."

I nodded and thought that, after that ordeal, it might be hard to sleep. Perhaps I would have nightmares about Mr. Headley. I had read that after traumatic experiences people often suffered from such things for a long time.

Once home, coddled by Miss Manley and administered pain medication and warm milk, I pulled my aching body up the stairs, undressed quickly and fell asleep the moment my head hit the pillow. There were no bad dreams, but there were spells of not being fully asleep but also not worrying about it.

The sun streaming through the windows woke me in the late morning and I was surprised I had slept through the normal early noises of the household. It was a workday, but I guessed John didn't expect me to come in. I sauntered down to the kitchen in my bathrobe and slippers and was surprised to see Officer Reed enjoying a cup of coffee and a slice of cake. He was just as surprised to see me in my nightclothes.

We stammered a bit at each other, me apologizing for not being fully dressed, he for seeing me in that state.

"How are you feeling?"

I cleared my throat and found that my voice was in full working order as I replied, "I think I am all right. Just hungry."

"That was a brave thing you and Mrs. Manley did last night. When I think of what almost happened to Mrs. Proctor…."

"Yes, Glenda certainly saved my bacon. What a horrible man." A thought came to me. "Do you think he had anything to do with Mr. Dexter's death?"

"Inspector Gladstone hadn't interviewed him last night as Mr. Headley was taken to the hospital."

"It wasn't fatal, was it?" Now I sounded like Glenda, worrying that she would be branded not just for assault, but for his death.

"The word this morning is that he had a concussion but is very much alive."

I sighed in relief and poured myself a cup of coffee.

Annie came in the back door carrying a basket with something from the market.

"And what are you doing up, Miss?" she scolded.

"Hungry and tired of sleeping, I think."

"Let's see," she said and took a look at what I knew were red marks and probably bruises by that time, although I hadn't dared to look in a mirror yet. She gasped. "There's a red spot on your eye."

"I'm not surprised. He tried to choke the life out of me."

Annie clicked her tongue in disapproval. "Sit down. I'll make breakfast."

"I think I'd like to eat cake if you don't mind."

My decadent breakfast finished, Officer Reed off to do his duty, and Annie upstairs dusting and cleaning, I sat peacefully until a tapping at the back door announced that John had arrived. He rushed in and gave me a bear hug, which made me realize I had bruises elsewhere on my body. He released me and sat in the empty chair.

"Now is the time I can officially scold you for being incredibly impetuous and foolhardy in taking on Mr. Headley." He was not teasing; he was deadly serious.

"That wasn't my intention at all. I intended to put the blame fully on Mrs. Proctor, who initiated her 'research' as she put it, really an investigation of what those two men, possibly all three were up to. You know, for a while, I thought she might have killed Mr. King, but as I got to know her better, it became clear that wasn't possible. She might be commanding and somewhat overbearing, but she took this on to make sure that right prevailed. I came in on it late and my motivation was to prevent something from happening to her."

"I never thought I would say this, but thank goodness for Glenda," he said. Then he added, "Aggie, this may not be the best time, but I have something to ask you," he said.

MISS MANLEY'S tea group met two days later and by that time we had got as full a story as there would be about what had happened. Her sitting room was packed with women, and we were buzzing like bees in anticipation of hearing from Mrs. Proctor herself what she had discovered. Conscious of being the center of attention, she took her time settling down, taking her tea and a choice of cookies while the rest of us focused our eyes on hers. Annie, who usually made the sweets and left early in the afternoon, was sitting in a chair in the hall listening in. Although Officer Reed likely shared most of the story already, she wanted to hear from the horse's mouth about the perfidy of the Commissioners.

A big sigh. "Well, you know from before the Garden Fair I had my suspicions about Mr. King. Yes, he was the bank president in Adams and knew a lot of powerful people, but there was

something so smug about the man as if he knew he was above the rules."

"Your friend worked for him, didn't she?"

Mrs. Proctor chose her words carefully, probably because she didn't want anyone to think that the secretary should be implicated or had been talking out of school. "Margaret is a very discreet and loyal employee. But again, I sensed something was not right."

I would bet Margaret told her fellow Daughter of the Nile more than either of them was willing to admit.

"So, I began to investigate. The County keeps detailed property records and transactions, and ownership changes are public record." A murmur in the group told me that many women there didn't know that. "It was meticulous work, but I was able to see that certain properties were purchased by a company that nobody seemed to know about. I dug it out from the files in Springfield where the Secretary of the Commonwealth has an office. And there it was. Mr. King and Mr. Headley were partners in that company. They were buying up land adjacent to places that were undergoing rezonings to take advantage of the increase in value. And then we come to the matter of the bridge." She paused to take a sip of tea.

I put down my teacup to rearrange the scarf I had been wearing around my neck to disguise what were initially red marks and were now fading bruises. The scarf seemed totally in character with my casual clothing but would have looked ridiculous with my nurse's uniform, which I was hesitant to wear because of the exposed neckline.

"The dilapidated bridge that the Commissioners were hesitant to fix. That's why Mr. King was able to get the nearby land for a song before he was going to push through the repairs or the rebuilding of it. So very self-serving. And once Mr. Headley got wind of what he had done, he was sure Mr. King probably had other irons in the fire. The partnership was structured in such a way that the one partner would inherit if the other died—and that gave Mr. Headley the perfect motivation to kill Mr. King."

We all knew that he had killed Mr. King by that point, but it still elicited a gasp and murmuring from the crowd.

When it quieted down again, she continued. "I just learned this morning that he was also responsible for the death of Mr. Dexter, who had done research of his own. And left poor Joanna a young widow with a baby."

Voices were now angry at the heinous deeds committed in the interests of money and power.

Miss Manley tried to get control of the group. "Ladies, yes, we know terrible things were done, but let's thank Mrs. Proctor for bringing this all to light."

There was enthusiastic applause. Her election in the fall to the post was all but assured.

"But we have two other heroines here with us today," Miss Manley continued. "Glenda and Aggie." More applause. "Tell them what happened."

Glenda and I looked at one another and by tacit agreement, she started the narrative from the time we finished dinner and saw Mr. Proctor out on the street looking for his wife. Then it switched to me relating the portion of climbing the fire escape and entering through an open window. Glenda picked up the thread of searching on the Commissioner's floor for Mrs. Proctor, finding her, hiding in the closet, my bursting out and knocking Mr. Headley to the ground.

"And while that vile man was trying to strangle me, Glenda picked up Mr. King's statue of Honest Abe—that's rich—and hit him over the head."

"What a story," Miss Olsen said with longing in her voice that she hadn't been there.

"That's right, it is a fantastic narrative. Stuart should write it up as one of his action-adventure stories," I said. "Only this could be a series for girls." I readjusted the scarf on my neck.

"And at the end, one of the heroines gets engaged?" Mrs. Rockmore said archly.

I looked down and noticed that I had my left hand at my neck and the diamond on my finger had caught the light.

My secret was out.

"Yes. That would be a perfect ending to the story," I said, holding my hand out so everyone could see. Now the applause was for me. And if I do say so myself, well deserved all around.

I predict it's happily ever after for Aggie and John.
The long summer's work needs a break and where better to relax than at Aggie's aunt and uncle's vacation home in Maine?
Unless there is a murder.

Find it here:

MURDER AT THE BEACH HOUSE

SIGN up for my newsletter to see when the next Berkshires Cozy Mystery is ready for release.

ANDREA KRESS

www.Andreas-books.com

Thank you! Happy Reading,
Andrea